*In Light of Chaos*

# In Light of Chaos

*Béla Szabados*

Thistledown Press

Canadian Cataloguing in Publication Data

Szabados, Béla, 1942-
  In light of chaos
  ISBN 0-920633-73-0

PS8587.Z33I5 1990    C813'.54    C90-097108-8
PR9199.3.S933I5 1990


Book design by A.M. Forrie
Cover photograph by Sean Francis Martin
Typeset by Thistledown Press Ltd.

Printed and bound in Canada by
Hignell Printing Ltd., Winnipeg

Thistledown Press Ltd.
668 East Place
Saskatoon, Saskatchewan
S7J 2Z5


Acknowledgements

Lyrics from "Weary River": Words by Grant Clarke, music by Lou Silvers © 1929
by Bourne Co., New York. Copyright renewed. Words used by permission.

This book has been published with the assistance of The Canada Council and
the Saskatchewan Arts Board.

The lover of wisdom has to descend into
primeval chaos and feel at home there.

- Wittgenstein

*For*
*Imre Nickolas Béla Szabados*
*my son.*
*1972-1990*

# NOTHING

1943–1956

# IN LIGHT OF CHAOS

"A true autobiography . . . is an impossibility;
a man is bound to lie about himself."

–Dostoyevsky

Mother has her hair in a *konty*, wears a polka-dot dress, joie-de-vivre. Me—shorts, young colt haircut—exploring the world of: Nazi soldiers by their tanks. They are smiling, happy to catch a glimpse of some life that reminds them of home—a woman, a child, even though he is just looking for a place to urinate and it happens to be their tank. The gaze of soldiers deprived of wife, children, family, friends, recreating the warmth of it all—none of it exists—retreat to a barely recognizable homeland. But, they take the Mercedes, shoot the chauffeur—the one we call Eggs—Uncle.

Beside the house there is a large park and a river. Huge windows and rocks protrude from the front wall, then the sidewalk. I hang about the trees in the garden behind the house. Cherries, sweet and sour, apples. Time seems to stand still. I recline on the branches and eat as many cherries as I can. The foliage hides me from view, but I can see out quite well. The beginning of an observer's life.

During a violent storm I am confined to the house. Afterwards I break out with a sense of relief and walk along the river bank. Ice on the river is breaking up. Suddenly—nothing. I am in the middle of the river, part of the river and its flux, struggling not to go under the blocks of ice. The current sweeps me down. Then, a dog, Bodri, drags me towards the shore. What happened? The electric lines fell on the ground during the storm and I stepped on a high-tension wire. Knocked me out and into the river. Unprecedented: I should be dead, they say. I do not yet know that such near-escapes are to become a way of life. My mother cries, searching for someone to blame, but can't find anyone and gives up. My sisters are astounded.

4

Mother is always away, working. When at home she is cooking
and baking. She is very beautiful. My favourite place is her lap.
There I can observe whatever is going on. I don't like everything
I see.

5

The drunken Russian officer, waving his arms, is looking for his
gun. He can't find it. Mother always hides his gun when he is
drunk and returns it when he is sober. He screams and yells that
he is going to shoot us all. Mother says the gun is in his room—he
is quartered with us, assigned to our house. I find the gun and
point it at the person I don't like. Someone stops me. I pass out.

6

Absence. There is no one to protect the women. Mother, Éva and
Edit, and Auntie Lenke. They do everything and seem to do fine.
But mother is exhausted—cooking and cleaning all day for some
school and then doing the same at home. Making preserves—the
aroma of cooking fruit. These delights are somewhat diminished
by the newly acquired puppy's ubiquitous excrement. I am in
charge of this seemingly uncontrollable animal, impervious to
my will. I give up on ever taming him. When I try, he cries, which
in turn makes me cry. So he runs loose and makes the whole
house his own. Unfortunately, I am told there is no food for him,
or for any of us. Hence he has to be given away—to the local
pub owner's son, also called Béla. And that I should go to have
Sunday dinner at my father's sister's house.

7

I would rather eat little or nothing than take food in an atmosphere of ice, where I am not wanted. I say this to my mother.
The sense of being a stranger overwhelms me around my aunt's

family, none of whom I recognize and all of whom I immediately dislike. My aunt, who has some affection in her, is an epileptic. She has sternly combed-back grey hair and shaky hands. Her sons, in their early twenties, stare at me as if I were an unwanted item that has been imposed on them. The husband is a sour and balding accountant. So I eat almost nothing at a table of relative abundance and given the unfriendly competitive stares I come to have an acute stomach ache. I vow to eat nothing. Death engulfs the house. I do not have much appetite in any case, which is just as well, for in post-war Hungary there is little to eat.

8

I take Mother's breads and cakes to the baker's for baking in the large ovens. It is a simple family but welcoming. White flour dust everywhere. Chaos, dirt: how can such fantastic bread come from such a dreary place? The daughter is somewhat older than me. Blonde. We stare at each other. The next day she comes to play. We hang around in the trees eating cherries and pretending to be monkeys. Then I fall off, luckily from a lower branch. She comes to see how I am. Frightened. Seeing I am all right, relieved, she gives a kiss. We go off to a hut I have built for a hideaway and she snuggles up against me. I feel a strange intensity, a surge of energy, explore her, running my hands over her and undressing her. I am surprised—why am I doing this? She is not so surprised, but I am astounded by what I see. She is different from me. The difference attracts and repels me at the same time.

9

A present arrives—a brand new soccer ball. It is from Kati, my twenty-year-old cousin from Budapest. In the park we play games with it, forming teams with the available boys there. At the end, one of the older ones says: I tried to climb this tree but I can't. Nor can anyone. Can you? I give it a try. It is tough, no branches for quite a while. Just the trunk. Finally I am on top. I shout triumphantly. No sounds from anyone. I climb down. Everyone is gone—also my new ball.

10

The kids in the neighbourhood have a home-made pedaller: a piece of horizontal board with two wheels at one end and a vertical board in the front with handles on top. I make one for myself and am in seventh heaven over my abilities. Speed is my aim. I push the pedaller up and down the sidewalk as fast as I can. It is a Sunday. There is an old woman in my way. Trying to avoid her, I start flying towards the front of the house—a sharp pain and I am out. I come to—blood everywhere. I can't see. Mother is taking me to the hospital. Only the intern is there; he says the split on the side of my head needs twelve stitches and could have killed me but for two centimetres. He is clumsy and repeats that he sews me up reluctantly for he is not really qualified, but everyone is out of the hospital. From this I acquired a scar which I began to like when I found that it bothered people to look at it.

11

Everything is mysterious to me. I don't understand anything. I take a watch apart and am unable to put it back together. I try to build a wooden airplane and it does not work. I abandon all forms of construction and seek refuge with the kids Mother calls hooligans, *proli*. They rob me of whatever I have, little though that is.

12

There is a confectionery just beside the ÁVO offices. People gather to eat goodies like tortes and drink coffee. I watch them; I like this idea. I go home and look for coins, the items with which people get these good things. Mother puts them in a jar. Finding some, I return to the confectionery. The woman behind the counter is surprised, yet willing to serve me. She has a warm smile and huge breasts—her flesh like whale-blubber. I ask and pay for diverse pieces of cake with a sudden unusual appetite. I am dimly conscious of this being not altogether right. I look out through the window and am looking straight at my sisters and mother, aghast at the spectacle I present. I am reprimanded, but it is not made clear to me just what I have done wrong. I am still in the dark. Money and its strange ways: it is everything, it becomes everything, yet it is nothing, just bits of metal. I decide money is bad and is to be avoided.

### 13

Rushing home from the park—I love soccer, am good at it and I understand something finally. The object is to get the ball into the goal past the goalie. You do this by passing the ball to your fellows, and if you are quick you rush off to the side bypassing everyone and shoot. We won, I scored three goals!

### 14

I am about to enter the house when I see a tall, incredibly thin man with large warm brown eyes deep in their sockets, looking at me. He looks very strange, as if he were detached from everything. Yet he does not feel like a stranger. He is calm and seems to know me, my name. We go into the house and Mother bursts into tears and embraces him. I am told he is my father. This means nothing to me. He has returned from Siberia. It is, they say, a miracle that he is alive. No one comes back from there alive. And no one comes back from there dead either. I don't understand anything and no one explains.

### 15

I observe him every day. He shaves. He gains some weight. At night he comes into the room and teaches me to converse with someone who is everywhere and nowhere in particular—

God: the sense-giver. He is astounded that I do not know these things at the age of eight. The sense-giver does not make sense to me but being with my father does. I still am nothing but am beginning to feel as if there is more to this nothing than before. He is called Béla. I am called Öcsi (Junior) but am told my name is Béla too.

16

I discover the swimming pool. My sisters, Éva and Edit, join the swim club and I tag along. It is wonderful. Lots of people, a feeling of freedom. I don't swim but watch how it is done. Since I am left to my own devices, I jump close to the side, grab the rails and get out. I continue like this and as my confidence grows I jump gradually farther and farther from the side, kicking and pedalling. My initial fear subsides. Astounded by my ability to act and do, I am thrilled and gulp down litres of chlorinated water. I have a goal: I'll be good at this!

17

My father is the city engineer. He inspects building sites and draws up plans. He has a horse and buggy and a driver at his disposal on certain days. On a Saturday he and I embark and go in the buggy to the slaughterhouse where he is given meat. The place revolts me. Cows and pigs are lined up and they are trembling with fear. Every now and then there is a gasp of death. There is a stench of death and excrement: the smell of fear. I try to vomit but can't: there is nothing in my stomach.

18

My father is proud of his acquisitions. There is little meat available, and whatever is, goes to Party officials and is gobbled up by the producers themselves. Chops, pancreas and brains. The latter two are Hungarian delicacies. My mother cooks them. Everyone eats, but I can not eat any of it. My father becomes furious. There is no meat to be gotten anywhere and he manages to get some—people would give their eyeteeth for it—and here is this spoiled mama's boy refusing to eat it. I do! A few hours later I am all red and flushed and am running a forty-degree fever, vomiting periodically. I am labelled fussy—*faxnish* ! But no one ever insists again, in spite of my incredible thinness, that I eat things I don't want to eat. I in turn become a hater of force and will not eat meat since I now know where it comes from and how it is gotten.

19

I love the horse and buggy ride and enjoy being with my father. So each Saturday I go with him to the slaughterhouse. One Saturday he does not show to pick me up. Mother is upset. They put him in jail. Apparently there was an accident on a construction site. Some worker fell off the scaffolding and my father is officially responsible until further investigation. He is let go a few days later, exonerated.

20

There is a quarrel between my mother and father. I do not know what about. But when I see my mother being slapped in the face, I put myself between her and him. I get slapped, too. Things subside and I retire to my room, smarting.

21

A conversation, a giggle between my mother and Aunt Lenke. It is about my father. Apparently he tries to perform at night but he can not. I am taken aback by this. What does he try to perform? For someone who is so able, why is he unable to do this vague performance?

22

Father is a mathematical whiz! Éva is given special mathematical puzzles at school. No one can do them, even at school, but Éva can after a few sessions with Father. He has a chess set—carved the pieces when in a forced labour camp in Siberia. The camp commander, a Russian, was also a chess lover. Out of the two thousand in the camp there were ten or fifteen chess players. My father was a grandmaster. He beat the commander—also a grandmaster—an unheard of victory. The games between them increased in number and my father's daily meal ration—a piece of bread and watery soup—doubled. He was kept alive to play chess with the Gulag commander.

23

They are all ninety-pound weaklings, falling by the wayside. They dig graves for their fellow prisoners and just about the time they are finished, half of them fall into the grave. No one has the energy to pull them out. He makes a razor and shaves—thinks of his family. When he falls into the grave he crawls out. Five years of just surviving. I hear this while praying.

24

He is know-how embodied. He draws up plans for buildings; he makes wonderful models of them which look quite real to me. For someone who is so able, it puzzles me that there are things he can not do. My heart goes out to him. Aunt Lenke says it is because he has been nearly starved to death for five years in Siberia and he is lucky to be alive. To boot, she says, he is already sixty-six years old.

25

My father uses a gold pen to affix his signature to report cards my sisters bring home. They are both very clever. When their report cards leave a bit to be desired, they forge his signature. They practice his distinctive letters and the way he blends the SZ into one shape. I see them doing this and wonder out loud why do they not use their own signatures. They spit at me contemptuously. I have never been spit at before so am reduced to tears. Mother comes to the rescue and stops the spitting. I don't understand why my tears prompted even more spitting and ridicule. I resolve to have nothing to do with my sisters.

26

Father is ill—he is being operated on. He comes home wearing a strange belt which supports his lower abdomen. I wake up at two in the morning, can't sleep. I look around and find him in the kitchen having a snack. He gives me some too. We eat a bit. He tells me stories about Siberia. Apparently the prison guards as well as the prisoners were starving. So were the Russians outside the camp.

27

Fishing in the nearby river, a neighbourhood kid and I make a rod and line—a wormed hook—and behold: I catch a fish which to me looks very big. I take it home and put it in the tub. I ask my mother to prepare it for my father. I am pleased with myself—and that I can do something for him.

28

He is back at the hospital. I go and visit him with Mother and my sisters. They won't let me in his room. The next day he is dead. I don't understand any of this. It means nothing to me. They can't be talking about him! I see him next laid out in a coffin—absolutely yellow in a suit. Motionless, smelling of chemicals and somewhat putrid. We all stand in a queue, each relative kisses him on the face. I do the same—though to me this is not him any more. The body, after speeches, is put on a buggy drawn by a horse. Then we follow the buggy to the cemetery in a procession, walking at a slow pace, or so it seems. Then the body is lowered into the grave.

29

He was a Calvinist—he took me to one of their masses one day. They all drank out of a chalice, ate and sang songs. I took part, but found it all discomforting. I had known him for one whole year; he was a presence—now there was an explicit absence. He somehow got rid of the Russian officers rooming with us and he made things more defined, clearer. There was a feeling of strength around the house. Someone who uses force can also protect. I understood this, but I resolved never to use force. My mother's tears were enough to teach me that. I decided I wanted to understand and explain—like he did.

30

It is summer. I spend all my time at the pool. I walk there in the morning with an onion sandwich. Practice swimming. The swim coach has two kids, one of them my age. We hang around together. After the practice most people vanish—go to work or what not. We are enjoying the eternity of time. It is so boring, we have nothing to do. So we sit and compete at who can sit absolutely still facing the sun the longest. This is harder than we thought. I become absolutely dark. My sisters see an Italian movie about Mexico—the altar boy reminds them of me. Dark, starved, thin Mexican boy with short hair. I am amazed that there is another who looks like me.

31

I store my onion sandwich in the cabin at the swim club. The sandwich disappears. Someone steals it, no matter where in the cabin I put it. The consequence is that I don't eat all day and feel faint by dinner time. I don't complain—it won't do. Although I become a technically first-rate swimmer, I lose the races regularly to the better fed boy with the second-rate style and technique. This irks me. I investigate to see who smells of onions. It is the huge boy who is a shot putter and is very strong. It is a losing proposition, but it has to be done. I am beaten badly on account of the onion sandwiches. No sandwiches and some physical injuries. So it goes.

32

I work conscientiously at my swimming. My sister Éva is the best girl swimmer. She is a striking blonde and very beautiful. Also a genius, but a kind, timid one. She has a bevy of admirers and her boyfriend who swims the hundred metres in under one minute begins to take an interest in me and my attempts to acquire better technique. He spends a few minutes giving me advice. It helps. There are six of us "frogs": swimmers under twelve. I love Éva—but from a distance—for we hardly talk and they always tease me when we are in a group.

33

Very suddenly I become aware of the older girls and their magnificent shapes and forms. This awareness is heightened by the games the older boys play with the older girls. A frog, when instructed by an older boy, is required to swim under water and remove the brassiere of the targeted girl's bikini. I do this; there is a pretended shriek of surprise and a quick retreat on my part. There is general applause and appreciation of the firm white breasts against the tanned young body. Naturally, this takes place only among the "initiated," after most people, including the coach, have gone home.

34

There is a sudden evening summer storm. Everyone goes home except the group and their "adopted" frogs. The beach cleared, bathing suits are discarded and there is splashing, swimming, chasing in the nude. There is incredible thunder and lightning. In the background, there is an asylum for the insane—barred windows—and commotion there too: frightened screams from the asylum mixed with the delighted screams of the young. A strange and ambivalent dissonance!

35

Some of the frogs become bold and adventurous. They strike out on their own and in a group in one of the cabins explore the body of an apparently willing girl. It feels wonderful, but the girl is not so thrilled after a while. Sensing her discomfort, I become uncomfortable and so do the others. We stop. The news gets around. The coach draws us aside and says: dear boys, you are coming of age and all this is natural, but it is not to be done to girls at the club or in one's sphere of friends. The summer is over and so is explicit sensuality.

36

I am to go to school. I have no idea what school is. I am given a pair of shorts, sandals and a short-sleeved shirt and sent off. Gloomy corridors; stern, serious faces; wailing, depressed kids; occasional fights. We are to sit down and listen. I can't do it. I get up and wander down the corridor looking for a door and fresh air. I do this frequently in the first three grades. Mother is showered with complaints from teachers.

37

The school is associated with a church: the church is huge and towers over all other buildings. We go in and stand around. Some events are occurring in front. I see some people go to the front, kneel and get something placed on their tongue. Suddenly I am keen to participate. I join the queue and later kneel and get a tiny, circular ring of thin pastry—tasteless. Some eyes are fixed on me, disapprovingly. It is our teachers'. Upon return to school I am accused of some horrible sin, and along with some other boys am given the strap. This confuses me further: what have I done? I try to figure it out, but nothing occurs to me.

38

There are plugs at the bottom of the walls in our house. My mother plugs in a lamp and the light comes on. I like this magic. I get pieces of wire and shove them into the plugs. Suddenly I can't move, scream, or do anything. It holds me—I am stuck to it. I hear Mother screaming at the door. She runs to me and detaches me from the plug. I am blue all over. Off to the hospital.

39

Our home is beside the river. On the other side is a park. There are stones in front. The rooms have huge windows and everywhere there is light. As you come in, you enter a large room where you can take off your coat and what not. There is a small bathroom for guests off this front hall. To the left, there are three large bedrooms. To the centre, there is the kitchen overlooking the garden. Pushing forward, there is a guest room on the right and also a cold room where food is kept and stored. To the left of the cold room is a large bathroom. A second floor duplicates all this but is rented out. On the third floor is the attic, where there are piles of sand. Mother puts pears and other fruits from the garden into the sand, burying them so they will keep through the winter. I discover this stockpile with my friend—the other Béla—and we eat a lot of them.

40

There is a large pit, the size of a city block, between the public pool and the city. It looks like it is made for a mass grave. Some boys play soccer. I join them. Running, as right wing, finally a pass, I am leading the ball when a mangy dog, foaming at the mouth, appears and attacks me. Feeling a bite, about to kick the ball to score, I kick the dog instead. It runs away, but I have a deep gash. Mother, cleaning it: *Rabies, rabies, that's the dog with rabies.* I am off to the hospital again. There is no serum at hand. They send away for it.

41

Mother paces all night. I feel good, tucked in her bed. Next morning the physician, stone-faced, grave: *If the dog had rabies, your boy will die ranting and raving mad, foaming at the mouth. Some dog bit two other boys. It had rabies. It is likely to be the same dog.* Mother: *Give him the shot!* Physician: *If I give him the serum, there is a good chance he will die from the serum.* Mother: *Give him the serum!* I am stiff with fear—paralyzed. I can not move when he calls. My fate is decided. I feel left out and already gone. Then a ray of hope: perhaps my father is waiting for me. Then again, the damp, narrow, black grave blotted out that ray.

42

I get seven shots, one each consecutive day. The syringe is gigantic, the serum like yellow pus. The needle is like a small knife; it is jolted into my abdomen. A silent scream—I hear it, no one else does. My father, I am certain, is impressed. It is dark and cramped in the coffin, but every now and then we escape, especially when our throats and lips are dry. We sit beside the river and plunge in to cool off. I hear: *If the fever does not subside soon, the chances for recovery are slim.* It is sunny outside and Mother makes her cure-all chicken soup. I have a few spoonfuls. It is good.

43

I am surprised. There is no food to speak of. We are not always safe. But I am happy.

44

We are about to go to bed when a group of uniformed people show up at the door. They are rude and aggressive. In the name of the government they "expropriate" our house and are moving us to a new place. They gather us and our stuff in the truck and take us to a one-room apartment where we live for the rest of our stay in Hungary. It is one room set aside for us in a house that had been divided up into several such units. My sister Edit is so frightened that she wets herself. I hear the label "reactionary" when Mother asks for an explanation. A connection, however tenuous, with the past regime. The world has become rather dark for me.

45

Our new place is dark, cold and wet. The bathroom is shared by other families too. The corridor leading to it is full of possible sources of attack. For a few days, I exercise discipline over my urges to urinate at night. But then I assert myself and brave the trip. I spar with the shadows and usually win. One night as I creep along, I see a shadow moving. I am about to attack it when I hear one of our neighbours, a policeman, cursing at me: he was there first.

46

The toilet is usually filthy. Since it is outside the rooms, no one takes responsibility for cleaning it. There is never any toilet paper. So we are to take pieces of newspaper along. The walls are covered with figures and obscenities written with excrement. Shitty graffiti. I want to escape. To get away I start reading whatever I can get my hands on. This plan is successful. I am in a different world.

47

I listen to jazz and English commentary on the Voice of America. The program begins with Duke Ellington's "A-Train". I love it. I learn to hum and scat it. The rhyme and nasal quality of English is seductive. I decide there and then to learn to speak this language. It is close to me. Its appeal is heightened by the jamming of the station by the Soviets. The reception is clear for twenty seconds or so and then there is a booming sound. Whatever little I understand of a sentence is interrupted and I am left to fill in the blank imaginatively—creative language learning.

48

Mother asks us to be careful with listening to the Voice of America (Radio Free Europe). Someone has informed the ÁVO that we are receiving it. From then on the radio is turned very low and I have a new feeling of contempt for our neighbouring policeman and his wife.

49

Friends of my sister Éva are arrested and sent to the mines. They are about seventeen and are caught singing American advertisements celebrating Coca-Cola—hence considered subversives. They also had a discussion club, critiquing the regime. Several months later the news spreads—half of them are already dead. Two of them have been shot.

50

Éva is brilliant. She gets top marks in the eighth grade. Yet, she is not permitted to go to *gymnasium*. The children of "real" workers—peasants and labourers—are given preferential treatment. Éva goes to work in a pharmaceutical laboratory and attends school at night. She smokes heavily by now and is often tired. I wish I could do something to make the situation right, but I don't know what or how.

51

Every now and then my sisters Éva and Edit take me between them and, arms swinging, we go to church on Sunday. The main area is packed with the old folks and quotidian worshippers. We stay in the side corridors. During the singing of hymns, someone strikes an obvious falsetto. I try to avoid meeting any eyes for fear of bursting out with laughter. The pious seriousness and gravity of the woman and the hilariousness of the falsetto eventually drive me running out of church and rolling with laughter on the first snows of winter.

52

Piano lessons: I want to play! On dark, starry nights, as I return home from the pool, walking by a well-lit house, I hear a tune; it arouses such passionate longing—as if I could crawl out of my body and reach the stars. Someone playing Chopin on the piano. Then a glimpse of a girl drawing the blinds.

53

I sit on a wooden bench along the corridor. There are five students in front of me. When my turn comes, I am stunned. I can not play! Inside I sing, hum with passion; outside, nothing but stiffness. Practice: dó, ré, mi, fá, szó, lá. We have no piano— no practice. The woman teaching me is indifferent. She sits and knits, then collects the money. I go three times, then I quit, not telling Mother. Two months later, having paid, she inquires from the teacher at the grocery: how is Béla playing? I haven't seen him for two months! The thrashing is painful. I pretend to stoicism.

54

I am beginning to enjoy school. I can actually stay seated, attentive and eager to participate. Dr. Budai is my teacher at Zrinyi János Elementary. This is my new school, named after a Hungarian patriot and statesman. Dr. Budai has a Ph.D. and he is allowed to pick his students—he takes them from the fifth to the eighth grade and then sends some of the lucky ones to *gymnasium*. He is tall, a man with impressive bearing and posture. Straight and thin like a wire. Perennial suntan, white clipped moustache, short, grey, combed-back hair. For the first time I hear someone with intelligence. Clear, articulate, he inspires enthusiasm and invites participation. I fly by the seat of my pants: I am winging it. Never do any work at home—it does not occur to me and apparently to no one else either. Yet by sheer osmosis and spontaneous performance, I excel.

55

My essays written at school exhibit a flight of imagination, ways of escape, and emotional descriptions that entertain Dr. Budai's daughter and the staff of a drafting firm where my sister Éva also works now. Éva reveals this to my mother and both are vastly amused. Yet there is a slight change in the way I am treated—as if I were somewhat odd, somewhat bizarre. I find all this embarrassing, but my pleasures in writing and exploring a terrain so near and yet hitherto so distant and far, are intense and I continue writing and reading whatever I can get my hands on. Usually the stuff my sisters read, *The Last of the Mohicans*, detective novels, biographies, failed lives, flawed love affairs, history and Villon's poems in the magnificently domesticated translation of Faludy György. Villon is for me a Hungarian poet. Up to now I have been part of the everyday life of my family, taken for granted. The new reaction to me gives me the status of a stranger in their midst.

56

On my way to school, a walk of six blocks, I see a girl, someone strikingly beautiful. Fine features, aquiline nose, blue eyes, short, cropped blonde hair. A year older than me, by the looks of it. She walks to school with her older sister. Their school is farther than mine but on the way. For several weeks, I just happen to walk to school with them, but at a distance behind, making sure I am not noticed. When I miss them in the morning, I am overwhelmed with a sense of longing.

57

Their home is a few blocks from where I live. Passing by I notice them all dressed up in bridal outfits—she as bride, an older boy as groom, her sister as bridesmaid and a procession of friends. They are playing some game. The boy has a white shirt and a red kerchief on, signalling that he is a Communist youth—a young partisan. Suddenly I have a sense of loss, of sadness. They are pudgy. I am thin. They are wearing wonderful clothes, I have one paltry outfit, mended frequently by Mother. And they are together, playing games that are entirely mysterious to me. To boot, this boy, a youthful member of the oppressors, friends of the crude Russians, oppressors of my family, has this beautiful girl! My sense of loss is even more acute than it has been. I decide to give her up and stop following her on my way to school. From then on I take a different route.

58

We form a Hungarian literature club at school. Dr. Budai reads poems and stories to us and we explore them. There are five of us. Three of us also take private English lessons from our mathematics teacher. She was at Oxford for a year or two before the war. As we do our vocabulary, the meanings of words become so alive that they almost spring at me. So far words and language were just ordinary, everyday bits of the world around me. That words of different languages can have the same meaning gives me a sense of discovery, something that I can not articulate. It is possessed of an aura of mystery and significance. Suddenly language and words are mine—I want to be me and also different. My English teacher says I have an American accent. It is the way I pronounce *banana* and *orange.* I do not know what these are, nor do my friends—we have never seen these exotic fruits. But their names have a fascination for us and set our imaginations working. Perhaps oranges are a bit like lemons—rare enough. And bananas like pears. These we know.

## 59

There is a really rough boy in class. He bullies the smaller ones and takes their things away. If they resist he beats them up. He and I are the tallest. But he is strong and muscular; I am thin, starved and sinewy. His bullying is beginning to enrage me. He picks on the boy next to me, someone close to me, and we square off. I have nothing to lose. There is injustice all around me. Mother is working all day, cooking for hundreds, cleaning toilets, and we are looked upon as bourgeois, as reactionary—as "privileged". They won't even let my genius sisters into school! And now this bully is bothering my friend for no reason at all. There are kids gathered around us. We box—I feel the blood running down my nose and taste it. But I feel no pain. I see his nose bleeding. The fight goes on. I am spurred on by this sense of fighting for the downtrodden, against all odds. The bell rings. Dr. Budai enters. Both of us get ten lashes on the buttocks and are to kneel in the corner for half an hour, our eyes fixed on the wall, away from our fellows. The bones of my knees hurt very badly; there is nothing to cushion them from the hardness of the floor.

60

There is a new teacher. She teaches us physics. She is about twenty-one, has a wonderful body and full breasts. They are the foci of my attention. I am in a world of my own where the laws of physics, of motion do not apply. I eventually look around and my classmates are equally enraptured. Those in the back seats keep their hands in their pockets and their faces are flushed.

61

We are on our way to the schoolyard for recess. On the walls, in awkward capital letters, I read: "The Principal is fucking the physics teacher—she is a fantastic, juicy fuck!" We are lined up and told to come forth if we know who did it. Then a direct appeal: he who did it, come forth; otherwise the whole class will be punished. Someone whispers to me the bully did it. I step on his toes hard, so he shuts up. No one comes forth. No one volunteers information. We are sentenced to run distance during recesses for the next three weeks. The Principal is young and irritable. He vows to find out who the "criminal" is. He is a devout party member and became principal over the heads of more experienced and qualified teachers. The older boys scream with abandon on the soccer field: but he is really fucking her. It was every boy's desire.

62

I am the bread-getter. At six o'clock in the morning I start standing in line in front of the bakery. It opens at seven. To begin with I am close to the front. But by the time they open, in the pushing and shoving, I am pretty far behind in the long queue. Sometimes the bread is all gone by the time my belated turn comes. I am particularly fond of the salted crescents—Hungarian bakers celebrated the ousting of the Turks from Budapest by creating this marvel. On my way home I usually polish one off. It is my reward for having gotten the bread.

63

On a particular Saturday I have an immense stomach ache. Mother won't permit me to go to school. She makes a special light soup and I am kept on a diet for a few days. I like this. By nature I prefer a five-day week of school. Although I have frequent stomach pains, I make it a point to have one each Saturday, hoping no one notices the regularity. If Mother does, she does not say so. My sister Edit, my constant critic, suspects something. My teacher in math and English looks up from her desk, surveying the attendance sheet, and remarks: Mr. Szabados, do you by any chance belong to the *other* religion? I am puzzled by this enigmatic remark. Perhaps she thinks I am a Protestant like my father was. Only years later, when I understand what it is to be a Jew, do I realize that she either thought me Jewish or she was being sarcastic about my truncated school attendance.

64

Éva and Edit become opera lovers. Vicariously, in a way. We go to see the life of Verdi, of Puccini—all Italian films which escape the film censor's hatchet. I also love the outburst of sentiment and the dark sense of failure and dreary death even for the immensely successful (if only in retrospect). So I extend my radio listening to the great operas and learn to hum some memorable arias. Some French films, with the actor and comedian Fernandel, are also shown. Yves Montand's *The Wages of Fear* is let in and is a big hit. When reading the *Nép Szabadság,* the government-approved newspaper, Éva notices a photo of Montand, a French Communist, in a voting booth in the French elections. She remarks: Isn't it wonderful to live in a country where one can *choose* to be a Communist. I also see my favourite: Gérard Philipe in Balzac's *The Red and the Black.* In these stories I discover that death and failure can happen to others too, not only to my father and family. Something comforts me about this, but then it further depresses me, leading to utter gloom. The thought is this: if it happens to us, it is depressing, but if it happens to everyone, it is utterly depressing.

65

I am small, in shorts, sandals, a shirt. Unruly, unmanageable hair, hardly any forehead. Mother says I look like a monkey. We go to Budapest. The train is crowded—long waits. The city is large, the apartments are tall and dark. The streets seem narrow and the buildings seem to tower over them and us. We stay at my mother's sister's. She has many rooms and mine has a bay window. I can not see out of it. I have to climb up to it and then look out to see what all the noise is about. It is a truck going around with men jumping in many different directions in the back alley—collecting the garbage. They are singing some phrases which I try unsuccessfully to make out. I ask my aunt later about it. She smiles and says: *they pick up various things, garbage, discarded things, and occasionally boys who misbehave.* I am terrified. I beg my mother to hurry so we can go home. She assures me that my aunt was joking. This is not humour to me. I do not see anything funny in this. I can see my father being "discarded" into the grave. My fears are not allayed, though I feel better in her lap, where I bury my face and blot out the world. The chant of the garbage men continues to run through my head:

Ószeres, Ószeres,
minden rossz gyereket megveszek.

66

I get an infection in the back of my head, just above my neck. It festers and will not go away. We go to the clinic. The smell of disinfectant is pungent and pervasive. It is chaos. People with various injuries, sitting if seriously injured, standing in line if stubborn or lightly injured. Emergency cases are wheeled in. The boil is cut and drained and bandaged. They are not possessed of local anaesthetic—I grit my teeth and refuse to utter or make a sound. In the process, I chew on my tongue and it bleeds too. But my self-imposed pain distracts from the incision of the surgeon.

67

The young partisans with red kerchiefs are marching up and down in formation at school. Everyone is encouraged to join. When it is announced that partisans will have two afternoons off school, a flood of us join. We march when the Principal is there—once he leaves us in charge of the Young Communists, we immediately start playing basketball. When I play centre I pretend to myself that I am a very tall black American. It pleases me to do so and I play better.

68

This private basketball fantasy is punctured by a photograph we are shown in class. The caption reads: How America exploits and discards its black athletes. The photo shows an old black man in rags, sitting on a sidewalk in New York, begging. The adjacent photo is of a young black athlete winning gold medals for the U.S. in an Olympic competition. I experience such violent moral outrage that I can't eat for days and my uncritical admiration for America is qualified. I keep on playing basketball as a black and now I am even keener than before. My dark skin and the fantasy give rise to the basketball nickname: Black Béla who scats Duke Ellington's "A-train" while playing.

69

May the first is Workers' Day. School is cancelled and there is a huge organized march celebrating the triumph of Communist workers and a demonstration against the U.S., the West and the Capitalist swine in general. We are to put on red kerchiefs and white shirts and start marching from our schools. If you do not show, it will be on your record. It is compulsory to celebrate this day—and its Protector, the Soviet Socialist Republic. Those of us who are tall are punished by special duties: I carry a big picture of Tito and some of my friends carry Eisenhower and Dulles. These are the arch-enemies and they are caricatured as mythical beasts—the bodies of dogs and their portraits—red faces—snarling and about to bite the socialist workers. Stalin, Lenin and the Hungarian Stalinist leader Rákosi, absolutely bald and corpulent, are the lights of these marches. Their placards smile on benevolently: on a crowd, some of whose loved ones are taken at night from their homes and sent to concentration camps by the ÁVO, the dreaded secret police, never to be heard from again. I am marching, my feet hurting because my only pair of shoes is not used to all this wear and tear. The rehearsed incantations are ritualized and strike us as completely meaningless.

70

A Soviet contingent, with tanks and foot soldiers, is going back to its barracks. The rumour is that Polish workers have rebelled and defied the government. This requires a show of strength. Small kids, some six to nine or so, march behind the soldiers chanting—in Russian—*jób foje matj*—fuck your mothers, mother fuckers. The soldiers in the last row turn and chase them away.

71

My English lessons are forbidden. The tutor has been warned that the teaching of English is looked upon as a reactionary political gesture. Russian is compulsory. Our Russian teacher is young for someone who was a prisoner of war. He has a Russian wife. He is even and steady, but his pleasant personality is no match for the intense hatred of the occupiers' language and for our resentment at having to study it. But my aversions disappear

as the course goes on—my love for languages is a potent source
of weakness of will. And when the teacher voices complaints
about the slow progress of the class, he singles me out for
excellence. I immediately take defensive action by making will-
ful errors in reading and conversation.

72

I join the opera buffs at school. We are rehearsing for Verdi's
*Nabucco,* to be put on in concert with the Railway Workers'
Union. I love the opera, partly for its theme—the oppressed
rebel—and for the wonderful chorus. It is a big success and we
are very pleased with the results.

73

Preparations are made at school for the summer. The best
student in each grade is supposed to be sent to a special summer
camp for Communist youths. I am the best student in my class.
I am summoned to the Principal's office, where the door is partly
open and I hear the words: *But Szabados is from a reactionary,
bourgeois family. He is not proper material.* Dr. Budai insists that
it is the *best* student who is supposed to go. I don't want to go,
but Mother says I should for  there is little to eat at home and I
am dangerously thin and undernourished.

74

We go to a resort near Lake Balaton. There are large tents put up
and we are divided into groups. Group members are from
various parts of the country, each group led by an appointed
cadre. Ours is tall, blond and cruel. There is a large common hall
for meals and entertainment. In the morning there is swimming
and gymnastics; in the afternoon there is "training our Socialist
youth for responsibility." This consists in the head-boys shouting
certain political slogans and us repeating them afterwards.  I
have a strong sense of not belonging here and request, due to

illness, frequent stomach pains, that I be allowed to return home. But, instead of this, I am examined by a jovial doctor, declared to be healthy and sent back to group activities. By now I have an aversion to groups—never any privacy, solitude; always with these slogan-screaming boys.

75

I devise a plan and resolve to put it into action, in spite of its inevitably embarrassing nature. After the meals, there is entertainment. People are invited to sing or tell stories. The songs are either Hungarian folk songs or Russian songs translated. The stories are from texts distributed at camp, all politically charged. I volunteer and start into the *Nabucco* chorus of the oppressed yearning for freedom. The Hungarian translation of this starts with the image of an eagle who has just been freed from the cage, spreading its wings, soaring. I manage to finish it off. There is dead silence. That very evening I am on a bus leaving for home. What relief! It is also a moment of triumph. For the first time in my life I planned something and brought it off.

76

My cousin Kati is visiting Mother from Budapest. She is very beautiful and very nervous and tense. Upon hearing my story, she gives me a thorough beating. She is all of twenty-two and Mother has to rescue me from her. But she keeps on muttering that I should make it easier rather than harder on my mother. I scream repeatedly that I would rather not eat at all than be in such camps.

77

I love Kati in spite of her occasional cruelty. She has wonderful stories from Budapest. The Hungarian film star and comedian, Latabár (often called the Hungarian Fernandel), comes on the stage in a crowded theatre. He is tall, thin, long-necked and bent forward. He has an elongated, rectangular face, flat as a pancake. Just to look at him is funny. He carries a large, framed picture. Whose picture it is can not be made out. He walks around muttering something inaudible, inspecting the walls. Eventually the picture can be seen. It is a huge photo of the Stalinist Hungarian dictator Rákosi. The muttering can now be heard: *Where shall I hang him? Where shall I hang him?* The crowd roars with laughter. Latabár is sentenced to three years in prison for the joke. And some who laugh too loud and have the misfortune of sitting beside an ÁVO security agent go with him.

78

My sister Edit is graduating. She is also clever, but is an epileptic, having occasional seizures. Her entrance to *gymnasium* is also prevented by the local party apparatus. It is systematic, inverse discrimination against the children of the bourgeois, against those whom they perceive to be "the professional class." Kati has an idea. Edit should go to Budapest with her, stay with her and work in the same factory. Kati is a smooth operator. She gets her the job. Edit is sad—cries for some time. But eventually she becomes a fantastic worker—a *stahanovist*—someone who produces the most, above the horrendous quota. A pretty bourgeois girl becomes the pride of the working class. But nothing has really changed, except now I am all alone—and I miss her even if it meant being spat at occasionally.

79

March 18—a great national holiday, the day of mourning for the Witnesses of *Arad*: the leaders of the 1848 revolution against the Austrians who were executed in the southeastern city of Arad. Blindfolded and hanged. The revolution was triumphant against the Austrians, but the Russians came to their rescue and the tiny Hungarian army could not fight successfully on both fronts. The school flag is at half-mast—and is black. A short "historical" speech is given by the Principal—he rewrites the 1848 events in terms of the Party propaganda. I rewrite it in terms of yet another defeat of freedom at the hands of the Russians. And they are here, visible, especially on national holidays like this when sentiment can run high. We sing the national anthem: ". . . this nation has suffered enough, both for the past and future."

80

The science text has it that the Russians invented *everything* significant. Mendeleyev certainly came up with the periodic table of the elements in chemistry. But, says Dr. Budai, contrary to what the text says, they have not invented the steam engine or vitamin D. His nicotine-stained lips quiver and his tone is critical. For a few days after this, Dr. Budai is absent from school. When he returns, he has black-and-blue cheeks and looks pale and worn out.

81

Dr. Budai announces that Hungary has gained entry to the United Nations. He speaks in glowing terms about the U.N. and especially its function to protect civil rights, the rights of man everywhere. But nothing changes. The men in the long leather coats and their Mercedes Benzes or Skodas, depending on their rank in the ÁVO, still pick people up in the middle of the night and make them disappear.

82

They chill and freeze people and places. Whenever they are spotted, people look away. When they enter a café, conversation, lively laughter, the sounds of life, subside. I walk by the ÁVO edifice each day. The sentry in front is an ordinary soldier. But there are cells underneath the offices. My father was interrogated for a week in one of them after his return from Siberia.

Debriefed. And the "conspirators" of Coca-Cola songs, they vanished in that building somehow.

83

I start doing gymnastics. Three times a week, three hours at a time. The skills, style, elegance demanded by a floor exercise challenge and exhaust me in turn. The routine is divided up into moves and elements; each of these is relentlessly practiced and then I orchestrate them into *my* routine—try to put some stamp of individuality on it, even in the compulsory exercises. I am too weak for the parallel and vertical bar exercises, but I learn to do a dismounting double somersault. While I am learning, my mentors, Béla Német and Miki Bertalanits, are assisting me. One of them needs to give an extra little push around my waist to complete the second somersault successfully. They praise my diligence and the progress I am making. One day I put an extra mat under the vertical bar and decide to do this daredevil manoeuvre by myself. The momentum is not right—it all happens very suddenly. I fall on my head—a straight headplant. I see stars, I see stars! I mutter, and keep on seeing them: bright little spots, scattered throughout the air for several days. The extra mat saved me, says the neurologist who examines me. Béla and Miki let me continue doing gymnastics on the condition that I do not engage in any of the dangerous exercises without assistance. This I promise heartily. I love the discipline, the practice and the readily observable results: a sense of accomplishment!

84

A year and a half later: the provincial championships for boys under fourteen. Our school team comes second in the group exercises. My floor routine includes a handstand and a subsequent roll to get into position for a run and a jump. The routine goes perfectly, except for this handstand. It is not that it does not go: it goes too well. I have had difficulties with it, but now the incessant practice pays too many dividends—I remain standing on my hands for about a minute, as if I can't get off them. I hear the sigh of relief from my fans when I finally tuck in for the roll. I win the floor exercises championship—my first triumph—but it does not feel a triumph. Almost immediately we get on to the task of ridding my routine of the flaws Béla Német discovered watching me. Some of these flaws I like and would like to work into my style, my routine. I am learning my own technique of survival: to turn flaws into virtues.

85

A very hot summer begins. The school assigns us a project—weeding railroad tracks for two weeks before vacation starts. This is hard work and it is harder in the hot sun. When I look up I can see the tracks running together in the distance. It seems a thankless piece of labour and a senseless one: yesterday's clearing is already invaded by new proliferating weeds. After eight hours of bending and weeding, we all collapse into a fitful unstable sleep.

86

Miki gets a job as lifeguard at a pool by the river, some distance from the city. Part of the river is dammed and a natural pool is created. I am given a bicycle by his mother and I carry his lunch each day, pedalling and loving the breeze hitting my face as I ride. I stay for a couple of hours and then pedal to the central pool and park to see my friends.

87

My target of observation and admiration is the old tennis pro and gym teacher, absolutely bald with the help of a bit of shaving, fit and evenly tanned. He is catered to and surrounded by two women: one very heavy-set with voluminous breasts, long, dark hair; the other blondish, somewhat stocky and the officially-appointed suntan-oil applier. She administers massages to both and then oils her own body with meticulous attention. After an hour's tanning, they go en masse for a dip, then have a bite to eat from baskets they brought with them. I am amazed at this well-ordered life.

88

At home, Edit is smoking cigarettes. I voice my disgust at this and start bending the little tin ashtray she made for herself. She asks me to stop and let her be. I am perverse. I keep on doing it and when she tries to grab it away from me, in the ensuing struggle I hit her. I know I have done something horrible. She is sobbing. One of her front teeth is broken off and the nerve is hanging out. I try to comfort her but she pushes me away. I decide that I can not be forgiven and leave home. I am away for most of the night wandering the streets until my mother and her search party find me. I am taken home. For the first time ever I receive a beating from her—a well-deserved one. I have to bend down and get fifteen lashes with a ruler. I feel I have lost my innocence, as if I no longer belong anywhere and no one really cares for me. Explanations are no good: I have done harm that can not be undone. I flawed someone beautiful—someone whom I love. When the dentist gets through with her, it still hurts her but there is also a clear difference between the insert and her own teeth. *Mea culpa*.

89

Again there is a sharp food crisis. Mother goes to the market each day and pretends to taste *one* green pea from each vendor. She gathers enough for some soup in this way. There are photos of women displayed on the windows of government shops. They are charged with hoarding food. Mrs. So-and-so's house has been raided and she possessed three kilos of flour and four kilos

of lard, etc. An enemy of the people! They are trying desperately
to find scapegoats for their failures: thus, mother. It is an atmosphere of suspicion: neighbour informs on neighbour and children are encouraged to inform on their parents. Do your parents
behave like good socialists should? Some don't, we hear in the
official rags. The hoarders publicly confess their misdeeds.

90

My gaunt appearance and hacking cough are of concern. I am
sent to the country, to my mother's stepbrother, Uncle Béla, and
his wife, Joli. He is a retired teacher and plays the organ for the
village church. The train from Szombathely takes me to a station
and the village itself is a ten-kilometre walk. It is horribly hot and
dusty. There is a drought. Finally I arrive. The house has a
thatched roof and a family of storks makes its home there. Their
beaks are long and yellow, their wings powerful. Their presence
is welcome: they are accepted, historically honoured residents
of the country, magical transporters of new life and babies. I stare
at them, resting and summoning up enough courage to enter and
find out if I arrived at the right place.

91

I do have the right place. The house was designed by my late
grandmother. It is wonderfully cool. The space is partitioned
comfortably and with thought for our needs. There is a huge
kitchen with a vast built-in oven where fresh goodies are baked
each morning. My first duty in the morning is to take an instrument (a piece of wood with a handle on one side and four wheels
on the other) and massage Uncle Béla's back. He suffers from
what appears to be arthritis. Then I go and fetch water from the
nearby well. Then breakfast and everyone is free afterwards—or
at least I am, for I disappear regularly until dinnertime.

92

The well is a meeting place for the women and a few youngsters. By means of a pulley, you lower the bucket deep, some thirty metres, and then you start pulling. Hard work for me. The women are attired in clothes that cover all of their bodies—including a headdress. They are all in black and all one sees are sculpted structures of wrinkles, instead of faces.

93

There are a few young wives, too. They are mostly in white and chat a great deal. One in particular is very attractive and smiles occasionally. Aunt Joli says that this girl's sister threw herself into the well last year when she was abandoned by her suitor. She could not get over it. Perhaps only too late she realized her mistake. Whenever I lower the bucket I expect to have some evidence of her; a piece of clothing, a part of her corpse. But everything goes as it should in this village near Pápa in Rábacsanak.

94

In the afternoon I retire to the orchard behind the house. I weed a few vegetable beds, but mostly sit in the top of cherry trees observing nothing, for nothing goes on, or dozing off. Every now and then I hear: Öcsi, Öcsi, where are you? This boy is so serious, yet good for nothing. I wonder what will become of him: a career of doing nothing.

95

The outhouse is a horror for a city boy like me. The excessive cherry eating induces diarrhea. I sneak out in the middle of the night to the outhouse. The stench of excrement and urine is intense. But sitting with one's buttocks exposed to the possible violence of insects, rats, diverse creepers and crawlers, makes for anxious moments of relief. On my way back I wake up the rooster and he attacks with a fury. I defend myself with a mild kick. After all, who is the chief rooster here?

96

The pecking order is evident. The cathedral forms the centre of
the village. Then comes the vicarage, then the teacher's house,
then the various farmers' abodes. Uncle Béla plays the organ and
sings on Sundays at mass. He plays Bach and Haydn and church
hymns. The sound of the organ is sonorous and booms through
the vast church, attended only by a few elderly people. His voice
is terrible and offensive. He plays the organ magnificently. I
wonder if he knows these things?

97

My two weeks of being fattened up are over. I gained half a kilo:
mostly on breakfasts, cherries and bread at dinner time. I long
to see Mother, my sisters and friends. Boredom and solitude
make me very keen. I am fond of Uncle Béla and Aunt Joli, but
I came reluctantly and leave with a bit of sadness and a lot of
enthusiasm.

98

Our swim team travels by train to Sopron for the provincial
championships. Those of us under fourteen are "initiated." The
ritual is: bottoms are stripped and one is struck by each member
of the team above fourteen. The strength of the strike depends
on the mood, personality or disposition of the striker. I do not
like any of this, but my fellows say they really feel part of the
team now. I have always felt part of the team—now I have a
painfully felt part.

99

We win the under-fourteen relays and my friend, the coach's son,
wins the fifty-metre breaststroke. My other friend wins the fifty-
metre crawl. I come second and am pleased. On the way back
we are coddled by the older girls and I comfortably fall asleep

in some wonderfully fleshy lap. Later on we sing songs and munch on sandwiches. I have the sense of belonging to a large family without politics, without tyrants, without ÁVO, without the bald eagle Rákosi. It feels good.

100

Edit barbers my father. It is a ritual. He sits in a large chair. She puts a towel all around his chest and shoulders. She prepares her instruments. Her movements are precise. She takes great joy in what she is doing. She cuts his hair very short in the back and on the sides. There are hairs sticking out of his nose and his ears. These spots require small scissors and delicacy of technique. She is excellent. I sit and observe the proceedings in awe. I am also conscious of observing love in action: caring for someone. She takes pleasure in caring for him, looking after him. I am in awe of this.

101

Uncle Béla used to wake me at six a.m. When I did not appear after ten minutes, he returned. I can still feel a flood of cold water all over me. It is a nightmare. I would sit up and see him leaving the room with a large bucket. *Automated douche*, he chuckled.

102

As I would walk to the kitchen I could smell the aroma of fresh baking. Aunt Joli was in front of the huge built-into-the-wall oven with a large wooden spade arranging her breads, croissants, rolls, eggbreads, rétes, bismarcks. Just the smell of all this overwhelmed me. I would polish off three or four items and walk around with a bulging belly. He who tosses bread away is committing a sacrilege, so the saying goes. I have no difficulty relating to this dictum of Hungarian peasantry.

103

Everyone smokes. Cigarettes are the opium of the people. My mother smokes two packs a day. My sisters smoke in secret. I go to the woods and gather leaves in the fall. Crushed, they feel like tobacco. I put them in paper and roll them. Then the anticipated moment of lighting up. A few puffs, violent coughing and subsequent vomiting. I brush my teeth three or four times to get rid of the dreadful taste. It would have been simpler to take a cigarette from Mother's package, but the memory of the theft from the vase of long ago still lingers.

104

It is winter and there is much wet snow. Miki and I set out for the Oladi hills—a few kilometres from the city of Szombathely. He lends me some worn boots which reach halfway up to the ankles. And we carry some ancient skis, flat wooden sticks, which are tied to the shoes just around the ankles. We slip, slide, fall. It is tiring and awful; yet as we wander home, our clothes soaked through with moisture, shivering, I have a sense, a vibrant sense, of being alive, of being in tune with trees, snow, water, and the occasional rabbit which has escaped the hungry hunter's trap or gun.

105

The Romans had been here. There are ancient roads unearthed: architectural mosaics in various colours, faded yet enduring. There is evidence deep down of their soldiers, collected from all over Europe, living, building here, guarding the empire from this far-flung outpost they called Sabaria. Dr. Budai is sure there are major archaeological finds yet to be uncovered. We dig deep and find strata of former life. Dr. Budai speaks for them, fits them into our lives, and enables us to grasp these ghosts. My milieu becomes mysterious, its inhabitants more numerous. I want to dig deep, yet not lose sight of the surface.

106

An inspector from the government comes. He goes to the toilet on the archaeological site. Sits down and in the pleasant stupor of defecation his eyes fix on the inscription on the floor of the toilet. *Ave Caezar Va Van.* He had a smattering of Latin. Archaeological inspectors are supposed to be good party members, not versed in history—they are to put an end to history. He jumps at this inscription and takes it to be a major find. He may be a party member, but he has not lost his curiosity. He rushes out past us to see the chief archaeologist: Comrade, how could you have missed this incredibly important find? The archaeologist looks at the "find" and coolly observes: But comrade, this is simply Hungarian, *a vécé zárva van*—meaning, the toilet is occupied. It is a story everyone loves.

107

My fellow swimmer and friend plays the piano. He chops away at Beethoven's "Moonlight Sonata" and a "Nocturne" by Chopin. We have a great dispute: is it Ludwig van Beethoven, or is it Ludwig von Beethoven? I say "von"; he says "van". I have taken up German a few weeks before. Having learned that "von" precedes German family names occasionally, I insist with conviction. It is a question of *who* is right. When it turns out that I am wrong, the futility of this absolute certainty and investment of the will comes home to me. I do not cease to venture an opinion, but being mistaken is liberating. We all learn every day, says our coach, who finds the dispute amusing. He thinks it is the music that counts. "Von" or "van" does not matter one bit. But we want to get it right: the first stirrings of epistemic thirst.

108

Searching for enlightment, I pop a big question to Éva: *What is the most enjoyable thing in life?* She looks at me with a melancholic smile and says: *Why, it's simple: having a shit.* Her pronouncement is deflating. I greet her answer with undisguised contempt. It is an uncharacteristic crudity for someone so quintessentially refined.

109

In the shop windows there are photos of women—some old, some young—all looking downtrodden, all accused of being enemies of the workers. They hoard food. The scapegoats for the food crisis. Theft at work becomes commonplace for no one can live on what they are paid. There is a radical shortage of all essential basic foods. Members of the Party apparatus, cunning peasants in the country, and Russian generals with their staff, are of course well fed, well looked after, rosy-cheeked. Mother observes: *If we the workers own everything, it is absurd to have twinges of conscience for taking a pork chop home for your kids. How can you steal from yourself?*

110

Botany, its taxonomy, its attempt to label the infinite storehouse of nature—I have an aversion to it. There are some glimmerings of truth. Here it is impossible to excel unless I really work at it. Luckily it is a brief course. None of my aversion diminishes the wonder, the order and geometry, of the botanical garden. I am puzzled when told that this is a botanical laboratory of nature. For me nature is wild, chaotic, surprising. Here everything is frozen for observation. In the midst of living things, I am overcome by a sense of death and stillness. I fear being caught, frozen and pinned for exhibition. It is momentary, this price I pay for knowledge. Then I feel at home in the botanical garden and visit often—as I do my father's grave.

111

My appetite is picking up and I am beginning to eat things other than bread, soup and the occasional bit of salami. I venture into mushroom soups and spinach purée with a fried egg and pieces of fried potato on the side. At one time the sight of this food revolted me. A deep poisonous green circle with a yellow eye in the middle looking at me. Now I eat it, though cautiously. It is dietetic, Mother assures me—there is no fat or grease of any sort in it, except what is required to fry the egg and potatoes. Anything greasy still makes me vomit.

112

I watch with amazement the peasant boy from the country, a fellow student. His lunch consists of a large piece of bread, amounting to half a loaf. He also has a huge piece of fatty bacon, smoked, and cuts pieces of it. He divides his bread into pieces, too: on each piece of bread he puts a slice of bacon. These are his "soldiers", he tells me. He arranges them in battalion formation on his desk at school—then starts eating them. Half-way through, the starved soccer players enter and finish off his battalion without his permission. Some have, some have not.

113

Some have and then no longer have. He is fat and has a good appetite—he cries like a baby. I feel sorry for him. I am beginning to take pride in *not* having clothes, food, much attention, or apparently a body. I am feather-weight. Possessions, Mother tells me, come and go like a summer cloud. We had a Mercedes, a chauffeur, two houses, a maid and jewelry. Now we have nothing. It's what you can cram into your head that has some value, she says. I vow to cram everything into my own head, and own nothing. I float; I want to be pure spirit. I develop a walk: as I step I almost leave the ground. My sisters say I am absurd and ridiculous, but they no longer spit and begin to look at me as a strange phenomenon.

114

Gloom and doom set in. Two of Éva's friends commit suicide. They cut their wrists and bleed to death. One for no apparent reason. The other's boyfriend is sent to the mines—this form of military service is reserved for those from "reactionary" families. It means tuberculosis and eventually death. The one with no reason sticks in my mind—becomes an *idée fixe* for a while. My newly acquired purpose in life becomes blurred and I start keeping an eye on Éva and Edit. If this can happen to the others, can it happen to them? I intend to protect them. I follow Éva everywhere, at a respectful distance, for a few weeks—then I get very tired waiting for hours outside the local Espresso house where she hangs out with friends for hours. Enough of this. She will have to take care of herself!

115

Three of us from the defunct Hungarian literary club keep company. Petöfi, the Hungarian poet, revolutionary and patriot, is a shared hero. He died young on the battlefield, fighting the Russians in the 1848 Revolution. He was twenty-five and his output was incredible—the school's library shelves are filled with his works. But a different note is struck by another poet, Ady Endre, an émigré who has lived in Paris and written there. His world is full of everyday, ordinary life, yet there is an underlying complaint and criticism which is both firm and gentle. A keen eye, a subdued sentiment which is easier to understand than Petöfi.

116

Now I not only see things, but I see them as something. The weight, the burden of disconnected experience is beginning to lift. For me this is like trying to find my way in a fog. Lots of patches remain, but the fog is beginning to lift. I have a sense of making my world.

117

There is a strange sense of excitement in the air. As if something were occurring of real importance. There is increased tank movement by the Russians. Dr. Budai hints at changes that are about to take place—reforms. Stalin is dead! The poetry of toilet graffiti covers the walls at school: *Misery and destitution, but a seven-metre Stalin sculpture, misery and destitution!*

118

It is remarkably hot in October. I go to school in shorts and shirt sleeves. My birthday is at hand and I am full of expectations. But if I am asked what I expect for a present, I can not say. I am going to be fourteen years old. But nothing happens. Mother makes doughnuts and as she makes them I eat them. I eat a hitherto unheard of number: twenty doughnuts. I have begun to expect the unexpected.

119

Crowds of people demonstrate in Budapest. Stalin's statue is destroyed by the crowds. Among the demanded reforms, formulated by the university students: the withdrawal of Russian troops from Hungary; democratization; release of political prisoners; and Imre Nagy as leader of government. So my cousin Kati whispers to my mother. There is shooting: it is a full-fledged armed uprising. The Russian tanks have moved in. Only the shoes, each three feet long, of Stalin's statue remain.

120

We are glued to the radio. Our people have taken over the radio. Gone is the gravity, the official seriousness of the announcer— there is a lightness of tone, there is hope. I rush outside and meet my friends. My own city is turbulent as well. There is a demonstration in front of the ÁVO building, about a thousand people

with the traditional Hungarian flag—red, white and green, the
Soviet-style emblem cut out. Német Béla, my gym teacher and
trainer, is one of the leaders. He carries this huge flag. The crowd
demands the immediate release of political prisoners. "Freedom,
freedom, freedom. Off with the Russian yoke."

121

Imre Nagy is Prime Minister. Political prisoners are freed. Members of the ÁVO are stripped and hung by their very ties by the
enraged crowd. The Russians accede to the withdrawal of troops
and democratization. So we hear over the radio. In the provincial
city where I live, these events are slowly reacted to. My friends
and I decide to hasten things. Inscriptions of "Russians go home"
and "Free Hungary" are our masterworks on public buildings
and fences. I feel slightly ashamed. Boys a few years older throw
Molotov cocktails at Russian tanks. I write political graffiti on
walls. We want action!

122

My mother's blonde friend, Aunt Lenke, goes berserk. Her husband is dying of cancer. In the middle of this jubilant enthusiasm,
this feather-light atmosphere, she celebrates by offering her
body to all comers in the public park. She is taken off to the
asylum, but not before initiating a puzzled youngster into "man-
hood". To speak of this is taboo.

123

The Soviet tanks roll into the square at the heart of the city of
Szombathely. There is a large armoured division here, for this is
a city a few kilometres from the western border of Hungary.
Austria is less than fifteen kilometres away. Vienna is closer than
Budapest. A curfew is imposed—we are all glued to the radio to
hear what is happening in Budapest. When we switch it on, there
is no program, but the steady, incessant playing and replaying

of Liszt's "Hungarian Rhapsody"—full of passionate grief, sorrow and suffering, a funeral march. We are burying a short-lived freedom. It is a dirge. Mother predicts: *No one will come to our rescue; the Americans won't risk war for us.* All prisoners are released indiscriminately.

124

The mines along the Austrian border have been lifted. Éva and many of her friends disappear—one day they simply vanish—and a sense of emptiness sets in. Mother won't say anything until she receives some message that Éva is all right. Éva escaped—crossed the border—and is in *the West.*

125

Confusion and uncertainty prevail, even in the family. Mother must decide: to stay or to leave—to escape and join Éva. She and Edit decide we must leave. I am reluctant. This is my home, my country. There is something to be done here. One can't just get up and leave. There are friends, teachers—yes, but lots of them have already left. There is no future here for someone like me. I shall end up in the mines—I can't even get into *gymnasium.* It doesn't matter if you're excellent. Haven't you learned from the history of your sisters? Mother sells her furniture for a bargain price, but in complete secrecy. Money must be raised for the guide who will take us to the border. No one is to utter a word to anyone about this. No one is to say good-bye to anyone.

126

At three in the morning we board a bus for a village a short distance away. We have nothing to carry—we own nothing—just some clothes on our backs. From the village the three of us are met by a middle-aged peasant. He is the guide, rectangular-faced, square-jawed. He takes us back to his house and demands five thousand forints more than was agreed upon by an intermediary. Mother is furious but has to agree: there is no turning back now, and this man knows it. I have a very bad impression of him; it is the same feeling I had at my father's funeral when I saw the men who deal in corpses. The price has gone up because the danger has increased, he says. They patrol the border with teams of German Shepherd dogs, at regular hours. He knows their routine and will take us close enough so that we need to walk only a short distance, fifteen minutes at worst, and then we are at the border and can get across to Austria. Mother pays up. I want to do permanent damage to him.

127

We walk, stumble and crawl for about an hour. Finally the guide says, pointing in a certain direction, *Walk straight ahead for about fifteen minutes and then you will see some abandoned watch towers. You will then be just a few steps away from Austria.* He takes the rest of his money and goes. It is pitch dark and cold—it is an early winter. We continue walking for three hours, cursing the peasant guide. Mother says: *The cunning of the Hungarian peasant is notorious.* She should know, being of peasant stock. But this is more than cunning: this is cruel deception. It is getting light—we desperately hope to cross before daylight. Finally, half-frozen, we see the watch towers. They loom in the distance like ghosts, warning, beckoning. . . . There is the faint sound of an explosion. Some unhappy refugee stepping on a mine that has not been removed. There is no patrol in sight. We decide to go for it now. Another half an hour's walk and we are in the safety of Austria. We collapse on a haystack and sleep. Waking up, I see a Red Cross truck and a woman coming to us with fruits, chocolates and sandwiches. There are others already on the truck—they are picked up along the border on a regular basis. Some people are wounded. I am still exhausted, but I have my first taste of an orange—and a feeling of glorious, absolute freedom. My euphoria subsides when I look back from the truck: I seem to hear some plaintive sounds—my father, Dr. Budai and Petöfi, all crying, and suddenly I am overwhelmed by a sense of grief and betrayal. I lie prostrate on the truck, unable to suppress my tears.

128

I keep on crossing this border for ten years. At night. In my nightmares.

# NEITHER NOTHING NOR SOMETHING

## 1956–1958

## IN LIGHT OF CHAOS

"You can't *really* tell it like it *really* is."
–Derrida, borrowed from a pop song

## 1

Austria: *Ungarische Flüchtningen "Lager"*. We are collected and transported in a bus to a *Lager*—a camp. This Lager is in Treis-kirchen about thirty kilometres from Vienna. It is a huge, neglected castle with barracks and it is to serve as quarters for us and about ten thousand other Hungarian refugees.

A dormitory, housing about a hundred to a hundred-and-fifty men, women and children of all sorts of background, is our home for a few weeks. There is a strange chemical smell throughout. It is the liberal use of disinfectant to prevent disease. Blankets and linen are issued to us and we get meal tickets for the enormous hall where all eating functions take place. The first night I can't sleep. I just lie there with closed eyes.

## 3

I am about to fall asleep when some guttural sounds arouse my curiosity. What I see astonishes me. A moaning blubber of white flesh, a woman mounted by a dark-skinned, mustachioed, long-haired gypsy. There is a rhythmic dance of sorts accompanied by a crescendo of moaning. She catches my eye and her pleasures seem even keener. I hear someone annoyed muttering: *Stop fucking around, some of us are trying to sleep.*

## 4

These nocturnal rituals of sex bring out the protective, censorial instincts in the parents with youngsters on their hands. Mother and the others request that families with children under sixteen be found different quarters. The Lager chief promises to do what he can, but it will take time!

5

Two men are quarrelling over the white whale of a woman. It is the gypsy and someone else. The woman sits contentedly on top of the bunk-bed and enjoys the fight. Knives are drawn and blood spills. Apparently they let out the thieves, the murderers, the criminally insane, from the prisons along with Cardinal Mindszenty and political prisoners. This act of violence produces results. Next day we are in a small but independent room—connected with the Lager's swimming pool. Mother is in charge of the pool. She and two others clean it and supervise swimmers. The odour of chlorine is pervasive and makes me nauseous.

6

Edit is working. She is sorting the various clothing items that are sent through the Red Cross, the U.N. Refugee Organization, for the Hungarian escapees. I am very displaced and bored. I spend my time exploring the camp. It has one large entrance with a guard's hut, and at the peripheries it is bordered by a high stone wall stretching for several kilometres. The highlight of my day is the single orange and chocolate bar I buy with money from my mother at the Lager shop. Then I try to read old copies of *Time* and *Life*, European edition. I can make sense of about every third sentence, but only if it is short.

7

I venture out of the Lager and I discover the world of the Deaf and Dumb. I listen to what people say and understand only the occasional German word. I can not express myself with my accustomed ease. I consult the quickly-produced pocket dictionaries, whose readability is somewhat dubious. I feel much diminished, like the animals. I am thrown back to the chaos of unconsciousness. I resolve to learn English, my favourite language, so well that I will be fluent in it. And then speak for all the deaf and dumb in the world. German is not my favourite language, but I acquire a German-Hungarian pocket dictionary too, for I yearn to have some rapport with my contemporaries outside the Lager. Lager life gives me a strong feeling of incompleteness.

8

We hear from Éva. A post card arrives for Mother from Montréal, Canada. She and her boyfriend Mihalcsics Gyurka, a fellow swimmer, will sponsor us. We are to apply for immigrant status at the Canadian Embassy in Vienna. Then a wait of eight to twelve months. Since my earliest geography lessons I dreamed of living on the westernmost edge of California, hanging over the Pacific Ocean. The blue patch of ocean, the white sand, those tall, full-bodied, tanned blonde girls in bikinis—a somewhat more feminine version of those photographed in *Life*—and I building my sandcastles until one of the most attractive invites me to play volleyball on her team. Now my dream is punctured. How can I go to Canada when I speak English, haven't I been told, with an American accent? Can I dream differently just like that? It is impossible to dream of being a lumberjack in northern Quebec. . .

9

An impromptu school is set up. There are about fifteen of us ranging from eight to fifteen. We do languages: English and German. The English teacher is a tall and heavy-set American with a brush cut; he has a wonderful deep voice and speaks in a slow, accessible way. He teaches us "through pictures". He speaks no Hungarian; hence, when the pictures can be interpreted in several ways he provides further clues by enacting the episodes. I am very impressed by him. He enjoys what he is doing. Our Hungarian teacher says that the American took a year off from university to help the refugees. We are preparing a short play for the end of the second month of the school year. I have a starring part, but fall ill with pneumonia. I do not even have a chance to say good-bye to him.

10

One afternoon some of us bigger boys are asked to help unload a truck full of coal. This includes a lot of shovelling and in the process we become covered with coal-dust and can hardly be identified. My sister passes by me without giving any sign of recognition. I revel in being incognito until the hour for scrubbing and cleaning comes. I am immensely tired from the shovelling. After four months without exercise, whatever sinews and muscles I had atrophied. I resolve to do regular, daily exercises. We learn a coalminer's song in English: "You load sixteen tons and what do you get / Another day older and deeper in debt."

11

Canada is magnificent! We gather in the immense hall to see some films on Canada. The vastness, stillness, ruggedness of the diverse Canadian landscape captivates me. The canoe cuts the quiet lakes like a knife. The Rockies' vast snows and the idea of grand, unfilled space makes me shiver with solitude; yet I feel: this is the place where I can do "something"; where I can contribute. A place which needs people. I wait until the credits appear, being the only one left in the hall—the National Film Board. I inject all my dreams, fantasies, aspirations onto the barren rocks of the western mountains. My inflated balloons and boats onto the rivers and lakes. I picture myself in the midst of the wheatfields, flowing—but doing what? I am there but have no definite idea what I am doing there. It occurs to me that this is like a film of a vast botanical garden—scrutinized in a distant way, as if from outer space. How can I make a place, a home, in the midst of such beauty? I would probably ruin it by leaving the wrappers of chocolate bars and the peels of oranges everywhere!

12

I have a swimming pool a few feet away, but go swimming in the village pool a good walk from the Lager. It is an Olympic-sized pool, surrounded by large patches of lawn, except in the front where there is a two-storey building. It houses the ticket collector, the showers and changing rooms on ground level. Upstairs, as I explore, I find a partitioned suntan area, half for the men, the other half for women. Everyone is stark naked. No young people at all, but an older lot in various stages of decay. The men are distinguished by pot bellies and war wounds; the women with enormous sagging breasts. I put on my new "triangle" bathing suit and escape from this cemetery of bodies.

13

Outside there is splashing and chasing; boys and girls my age play in and out of the water. There is a whiff of chlorine. I dive and start doing lengths until I am tired. I am just about to stop when I collide with someone: it is a girl with blonde curls, sparkling blue eyes and fantastic freckles. I mutter the expected "excuse me" and so does she. She notices my accent and my awkwardness and asks if I am a refugee. *"Ja ich bin Ungarische Flüchtning."* She joins her friends and I assume my sun-worshipping posture. They are well prepared for a picnic: baskets of food are produced and they have lunch. I have not brought anything, so I am starving. The girl walks over and invites me to join them. Wolfing down a few sandwiches, I try to say a few things—but alas, when they speak, and they do with enthusiasm, I understand little. Eventually I am reduced to silence and become a mere spectator. Very frustrating.

14

Next we have races and relays for fun. I come with a prepared text. When I track the girl with blonde curls under water and we both come up for air, I cunningly have my lips brush against her freckled nose and say in German, "I love your freckles." She laughs cheerfully, and kisses me on the nose as if I were her brother. However, one of the boys becomes cool towards me and I feel the ice in his remarks and behaviour: it is the boyfriend, I discover. Henceforth I keep a low profile and bring some friends from the Lager to be with.

15

I burn to find out where they go to school. I ask. It is a *gymnasium* some twenty kilometres away. I go there by bus. I walk around the school and then enter and present my application for admission to the secretary. I am told that this is a private *gymnasium* and not a school for "Ungarische Flüchtning". Rejected, I return to the Lager. I have sensed an expression of contempt in her behaviour at the school which I can not account for.

16

Absorbed in my English studies, I come across the phrase "blind date" in a *Time* magazine. My dictionary gives the following two entries in Hungarian: 1. *A rendez-vous between two parties where one of them does not show up.* 2. *A date who is blind.* Neither definition makes sense. I am puzzled and seek advice.

17

There is a Welshman who runs a rug-weaving enterprise in the Lager. He has a small makeshift building. His hair is dark and he wears thick-rimmed spectacles. There is a whole list of little difficulties I have. He is slow-spoken and very clear in his pronunciation. He sets me straight in no time. When I come to the "blind date" problem he chuckles with delight. He tells me that neither of the given meanings is correct. A blind date is a date whom you have not met before; whom you did not know before the rendez-vous. He invites me to look around and compliments me on my pronunciation.

18

I enter the room next to his office and see about half a dozen looms; they are being worked on by women assiduously weaving and singing songs. The rugs have attractive patterns and brilliant colours: blues, yellows, autumn reds, browns and golds. Some adorn the walls. I am shocked into an awareness of the world of colour. It is as if hitherto I have been colour-blind. For until now I have not had a sensation of colour. I feel exhilarated, alive, as if these new sensations are running through my veins. The women's songs melt into a curious cacophony: some sing *schlagers*, some folk songs, and others just hum their own melodies. There are three other rooms, equally charming. The women are my mother's age, forty to forty-five; they look very skilled.

19

There is a feeling of aimlessness and ennui that sets in. I feel bored and I am not getting anywhere, nor do I have any idea where I want to get. The mental fog that I so recently struggled out of threatens to envelop me again. I long for my friends.

20

I am hanging about the rug and tapestry weavers, watching their rhythmic movements as they slide their shuttles from right to left. Their songs, in which I now detect a new Western strain, lull me, pacify me. I sit, legs up in a corner on the floor, with a copy of *The Old Man and the Sea* and my two dictionaries. I read one of Hemingway's naïf sentences—pithy and powerful. I try to imagine, from understanding half the sentence, what he could mean, how I could complete it. Then I go to the dictionary to dig up the words. Sometimes what I imagine is correct and fits. Sometimes it does not. A pleasant surprise. It makes me feel I half-understand the man.

21

The Welshman calls me, interrupting my translating reveries. He needs help in his communications with his Hungarian associates and employees. His interpreter has just left for the U.S.A. Would I help out until he gets another one? He would pay too, as much as he can afford. I am pleased at the offer, for I feel the need to do something constructive. I take on the job of being his "translator" for a few hours a day; his "official interpreter".

22

He speaks very clearly, but some of the subject matter is highly technical—at least for me. I do not possess the vocabulary of accounting, business transactions and weaving. So I frequently feel frustrated. My efforts at rendering a thought, a request, an order, bog down. This is not uncommon. But then there is the occasional triumph of a successful exchange. These occasions become more frequent for I am learning a great deal.

23

There are new faces at the office of the Welshman. His associates arrived from London: a tall mustachioed Spaniard and his half-sister. She has short, dark hair, bright brown eyes, an aquiline nose and high cheekbones. Half-Spanish, half-English, I am told. Love at first sight—on my part, that is. She is immensely helpful. She gets me a comprehensive dictionary and we compile the frequently used terms in transacting the business of the office. Each evening I go at these words and their uses. Things go much better. I become less frustrated as an interpreter, but more frustrated with the burden of an intense desire for her.

24

Pay-day. I am surprised by what seems to me such a large sum of money. I give half of it to Mother and with the other half I want to send a parcel of gifts to Dr. Budai: a razor, blades, chocolates, fruits and various items that are virtually impossible to obtain in Hungary. Edit purchases all these things. Now we have a problem: how to send this parcel without compromising him in the eyes of the authorities? The ÁVO looks every gift horse in the mouth.And the reaction to the revolution has made things much worse. Mother says it is best to send it through CARE, an anonymous gift-sending agency: you specify what you want sent, pay the estimated sum and they, through an agreement with Hungary, guarantee delivery. Source of funds—"a former student." Edit and I eat the oranges and chocolates we recently bought.

25

I use the razor to shave myself. The act of shaving is no longer avoidable. The slight fur on the sides of my face is replaced by cuts and gashes—this business of shaving is an art, it takes time and care. After a week of quick, raw shaving, I decide to cultivate this art: soften up the skin, lather it, then shave downward and later, if needed, upward for a fine shave. So I am told by the smooth-shaven bullfighter Spaniard. I use the soap to soften the skin. Therein lies the problem, he says. Next day he gives me a special shaving soap and brush. Much better.

26

My days as official misinterpreter are over. I welcome the arrival of the new interpreter with a sense of relief. Seeing this and my keen efforts at competence bound to failure, my Spanish-English mentors cook dinner for me—paella. They also have their quarters at the Lager. The walls are full of Manuel's and Dolores's paintings and rugs. They both paint, both attended art school in London. I feel very much at home with them and their paintings feed my newly discovered appetite for colour.

27

A picnic with Dolores; we are speeding through the countryside in a VW. Our objective: the nearby hills. After a while we proceed by foot, climbing to a spot which affords a good view. There are canvases, paints, oils, pigments, brushes, palettes—I watch her painting and then carry on myself, improving and varying a bit on what she is doing. She praises my efforts and the final work is quite pleasing. Then we have lunch. Afterwards, I feel tired and take a nap. I dream of Dolores—of taking off her blouse and fondling her bare breasts—exploring further. . . and then I have this sharp, burning, pleasurable/painful sensation—and wake up. Dolores is packing things up and soon we are on our way back to the Lager.

28

A letter for me at the Lager post office. It is from Dr. Budai. Thanks for the parcel of goodies; and he instructs me to be "always a good Hungarian boy, to retain the language, to remember the great suffering of the past, and carry the torch for humanity." I know right there and then that I am given an impossible task. How can I stay and be a boy? Always? And to be a Hungarian boy in the West, in a locale where people have their being in different languages, traditions, who do not even know that the Hungarians defended Vienna and Europe from the Turks, losing a third of their population in a fight going on for decades? At Pécs, where the battle was a draw, the sky was red with blood! How can one be a Hungarian boy somewhere where people have never heard of Petöfi? I resolve to remember the past, to let the ghosts hovering over it haunt me, and to do something for humanity—I don't know what—but I can't do the first. It is an absurd piece of advice. In spite of its absurdity, yet again I have a sense of betrayal as I think of Dr. Budai, his students decimated in number, scattered across the globe, their children having names they can't even pronounce.

29

I get a new item of clothing. It is a summer jacket, light, no lining.
It is a perfect fit, clean and nicely wrinkled. I hate new clothes—
they look so detached from humans, as if they had a life of their
own. I find a little note in one of the pockets. It says in English:
"Dear refugee, we hope the jacket fits and you get years of good
use out of it. We are two schoolteachers who admire your nation
and your brave spirit. If you are ever lonely, please write to us
and we can correspond." I refer to my dictionary to look for
*correspond,* etc. Otherwise I understand the letter. It is from
Norway, from Oslo. I am enthusiastic and my imagination is wild.
I am grateful and moved. I compose my first letter in English—or
rather write with spontaneous exuberance, and then with the
help of the dictionary rewrite it. I decide to censor some of the
wild stuff: that I should like to meet them, possibly visit them;
that like them, I come from nomadic, marauding tribes; the blond
Vikings need not be scared of the dark, ferocious Magyars. . .

30

A visit to Vienna; at the Canadian Embassy we are examined by
the physician, fill out questionnaires and declare our intention
to immigrate. Vienna's buildings look grey, in various states of
disrepair. But the garden and the Palace at Schönbrunn I delight
in. Edit and I go to see the Opera House. Summer set in—the
season is over. Nothing is going on, we are told.

31

There is little to do, so I explore the outskirts of the huge Lager.
As I walk, far away from the barracks and main buildings of the
castle, I bump into three men carrying large parcels on their
backs. They want to send these parcels to their relatives. Would
I help them to lift these and carry them over the wall? They scale
the walls and I hand them their packages. Suddenly we are
surrounded by the Lager police. Despite my protestations, they

put me in the dungeon of the main administration building, along with the others. The chief police guard is fat, has a beer belly, a red, flushed face, and looks terribly indignant. His attitude completely puzzles me.

32

The dungeon is wet and dark and I am there for a whole day without food or drink. Then the door opens and the three men are taken by the city police and I am in the company of Edit, to appear before the director of the Lager. Through a German-speaking interpreter, I tell my story; the sergeant smiles incredulously. The director says that the other three will be charged with theft, or larceny, while I will be charged with being an accomplice. Edit has a tongue on her; she is furious. She retaliates by insisting that unless the director guarantees dropping charges against me, she will expose a conspiracy of a group of Austrians and Hungarians who take the best items sent by relief agencies to the refugees and sell them outside the Lager. The director's face drops and his whole manner becomes conciliatory. He promises to do what he can for me. I am dumbfounded: an act of kindness lands me in a wet dungeon in the free West. And here there is nowhere to escape. How can one escape from freedom? I finally acquire a sense of humour.

33

Mother is planning something. This whole episode convinces her that Lager living is unsuitable for someone as young as me. Finally she finds a private *gymnasium* for me. It is in the Austrian Alps, very close to the Italian border, near Innsbruck. It is an all-Hungarian school: they teach the whole range of subjects including English and German. The school is funded by the Dutch Royal Family, Juliana has been known to visit the place. I send off an application and my last report card from grade seven—grade eight is missing entirely. I am accepted and will travel to the Alps in September.

34

Whisked to Vienna for the trial. I am apprehensive, and the Austrians in their bureaucratic apparatus are easily imagined to be former Nazis. Mother laughs—some of them are, but most of them are not. She herself is of Austrian extraction—her maiden name is Niedermeyer. The magistrate asks me a few questions and it is all over with. An investigation reveals that there is indeed a large smuggling operation in the Lager. I have been vindicated.

35

I meet two people who work for the weaving Welshman. They are curious about me. They ask: You are Jewish, aren't you? When I say that I was baptized a Catholic, they smile understandingly and say: How else would you speak another language? This drives home the concepts of stupidity and prejudice. Mother offers rare advice: Ignore people and questions like that. She herself was mistaken for a Jewish woman because of her striking aquiline nose. Certainly not for her linguistic skills— Hungarian is the only language she speaks and her tongue is not flexible enough for foreign sounds, she says!

36

In 1943, two absolutely frightened women appeared in front of our home in Kolozsvár, ringing the bell. One, the mother, was old and crying. The daughter said: We are Jews and the Nazis are rounding everyone up. We live in that nearby apartment house. Hide us. And she showed a small bag full of jewelry. Mother brought them in and hid them. Later on, Gestapo showed up: Are there Jewish escapees here? No there aren't, was the answer. The man clicked his heels and went on his way. Mother refused the offer of jewelry, saying: You will need these in the future and I have enough of my own. Edit remembers this incident.

37

There isn't much to pack for the trip to the Alps. My favourite
Norwegian jacket, two shirts, a pair of trousers, shorts, pajamas
and a heavier jacket for the winter. Reluctantly I set out for the
railway station, promising to return as soon as I get a telegram
from them to the effect that we are ready to set out for Canada.
I have a third-class ticket, the cheapest, and an acute sense of
increased freedom. I stick my head out of the railway car's
window and breathe in the fresh air. A few inches away, there
are posts. The added danger makes me even more exhilarated.
I can almost feel them zooshing by.

38

Third class is crowded. I decide to explore the train. Crossing
from car to car, I find the diner and have a hot chocolate. On my
way back, I see that the compartments are empty. I pick one for
myself and soon I am lulled to sleep by the recurring clatter of
the train. When I awake, we are already deep in the mountains;
snow in the near distance and a chasm close by. Going into and
out of long tunnels.

39

The shrill, guttural German of the ticket-collector demanding my
ticket and glaring at me suspiciously. His suspicions are well-
founded. He orders me to return to third class, mutters about
foreigners who want to travel first class on a third-class ticket. I
am pleased: there is room at the top. These functionaries, they
are everywhere—to be ignored if possible.

40

At Innsbruck I transfer to a local line. Meanwhile my bag is lost.
I report it lost and press on. Some time later, I arrive at a small
village in a valley, surrounded by snow-covered mountains. It is

late. The station attendant says that the only way to get to the school at this time is to walk. It is a half-hour's walk from the village, on the mountainside. It is chilly but pleasant. I start walking and then climbing a bit; various *auberges* are built into the mountain by the road. And sometimes there are surprising, sudden gaps with sufficient space for farming on a small scale.

41

Three large chalet-like buildings appear; they are so picturesque that I stop and gaze for a little while. I go to the largest one. All is quiet. There is only a stocky, strongly built man in his early thirties. He welcomes me, puts me into a little room for the night and gets me a sandwich and milk. I wolf them down and soon am asleep, safe in my new-found haven high in the mountains.

42

The sound of a bell; very soon after, the lively voice of the man who welcomed me rings out: *Reveille, reveille, it is six o'clock!* The routine is: up at six; breakfast at seven; school at eight until twelve; lunch; and school again until three; a "breather" until four-thirty. A study session until dinner, which is at six. Then the time is our own. This is the blueprint for life at Queen Juliana's *gymnasium* for Hungarian boys and girls.

43

The dining hall has many long, large tables. Each room has its own table. Boys are separated from girls. Each day a different boy is the head boy: he is the one who serves the teacher assigned to sit at the head of our table. The food is wonderful. I am especially fond of the breakfasts and desserts. Pancakes with strawberry jam (crêpes Suzette) is my favourite breakfast, bread-pudding my favourite dessert. These Austrain mountain women cook up a storm for us.

44

There are six of us in a room. I am issued linen and blanket. One of my roommates is appointed evening raconteur—he delights in telling horror stories after lights are out. Unused to the early morning rise, I collapse into bed and fall asleep. Apparently he tried his best horror stories for the new boy—and I showed no reaction. He says: *He must be insensitive or very cool.*

45

"Réveille"—and the sound of the bell; and a shout, perhaps a command. I am only half-awake. Then silence. And suddenly a douche of ice-cold water all over me in bed. Jumping out of bed, I see the gym teacher and official welcomer, Mr. Horváth, surrounded by my roommates: *Szabados, "reveille" means "get up" and, as you see, if you don't, I am here to make sure you do.* He says this with a friendly, benevolent smile. Later on, he tells me that this is routine business; it happens to every new boy. Nothing personal. I take it very personally. How else is one to take it? It drives home a lesson: the place is rule-governed. I decide to adapt: I shall become *magister regulae ludi*—master of the game!

46

The classrooms are housed in the third chalet. This is smaller and it has a recent, makeshift quality about it. But the windows are huge and I love the morning light streaming in. It inspires me to perform academic feats like memorizing classic German and English poems and stories—Heine's "Lorelei"—we also sing. I memorize Milton's "On His Blindness", and some sonnets by Shakespeare.

47

One of my two favourite room-mates is blind in one eye. Attila. He has pitch-black hair, carefully parted on the side; a stubborn lock threatens to block his vision from the other eye too. He is quiet, assured and intelligent, with the looks of a military hero— someone who just came home from the wars—which he did—a maker and thrower of Molotov cocktails at Russian tanks.

48

We have very few textbooks. The teachers and the library have a few copies. Hence, there is much scribbling and note-taking; in the afternoon discussions and tutorials. It is impossible to excel by wits alone. But then it won't do to look too industrious, so I sneak off in the evening to do some extra studying. Some empty rooms are useful, or the library, or if it is very late, one of the bathrooms. One night as I open the door of the bathroom to do my owl routine, I come across a boy masturbating furiously, his gaze fixed on some picture cut-out. I apologize for disturbing him. His embarrassment is embarrassing. I have dreams of Dolores and wish for the understanding of the heavy-set Austrian matrons who collect my spotted sheets.

49

The girls' dormitory is located in the second large chalet at a fifty-metre distance from ours. Each morning they walk for breakfast to our chalet where the dining hall is. They have a school uniform consisting of a short tartan skirt, a white blouse and a dark jacket. I love to look at their fresh faces, listen to their lively laughter and try to catch snippets of their chatting. Their occasional meaningful stares lend a certain aura to their talk— intimate gossip, observations, etc. I pretend to be an absolutely bored observer with a wooden, expressionless face—simply part of the dining hall furniture. I begin to be comfortable with this posture of the cool, benevolent observer.

50

I am munching on crêpes Suzette—spreading jam on one and rolling it up, mentally rehearsing "Lorelei", which we need to recite in class today:

*Ich weiss nicht was soll es bedeuten. . .*
*Dass ich so traurig bin. . .*
*Ein Märchen aus uralten Zeiten. . .*
*Das geht mir nicht aus dem Sinn—*

and then I look at the incoming girls. My newly acquired, comfortable posture is punctured! The maid of olden times is none other than the girl who lived in my neighbourhood, whom I followed to school every day and who conducted her marriage ceremony over and over again with her sister as her bridesmaid and her friends arranged in a wedding procession. Her sister is by her side, now as then. Dark, refined and serious, this sister of hers. Now she is much more appealing than her blonde, freckled companion. I nod and they smile warmly. It dawns on me with a sharp twinge of conscience how I miss my sisters and mother. Until then I have not even thought about them. I purchase a card and, belatedly, report back to Mother about the state of affairs. I mention the Fekete girls in passing.

51

On the weekends we go on mountain hikes with a local guide. The small valleys, the little meadows contrast sharply with the huge mountain peaks. Balázs, red-haired and cunning like a fox, pretends to have injured his ankle. Attila and I immediately offer to take him back. On the way, we settle in the dining room of a homely *auberge* and spend our allowance on Wienerschnitzel and beer. I eat the Wienerschnitzel with gusto and drink a bit of beer with disgust.

52

There is an "adventure day" in the late fall. My room-mate and I take ropes and fix them to the third-floor windows of the girls' dormitory and climb up. The preparations take us some time, hence the element of surprise is missing. We are expected. As I look in through the window, there are two girls: one painted pitch-black, in white panties and brassiere; the other, pale-white in black lingerie. As soon as they see me they undo their brassieres and thrust themselves forward provocatively, then laugh and run through the open door out of their room. I let myself slide on the rope down to the ground, where the directress of the girls' dormitory tells us that there are limits to "adventure" and we have just reached them.

53

Sundays at seven a.m. there is the Mass we are expected to attend. We alternate as altar boys. Dazed and half-asleep, we respond *Christe Eleison* to the priest's *Kyrie Eleison*, with the automatism of robots. My fear is that of tripping with the gigantic Bible which I reposition at a crucial moment in the ritual. I genuflect with it carefully and then posit it, with relief. Father István calls us at the end—he is very discerning, suspects that some of us mutter the Latin, either because we have not learned it or have forgotten it. He will do Latin with us on a regular basis. No one is impressed by this act of self-sacrifice.

54

Skiing again. We don't need to go far, just a shot away. First, upon instructions from Horváth, the gym teacher, we build a snow wall between the road and the end of the ski run. We work our way up the hill and then, ignoring all advice, speed downwards, laughing away the fear of being unable to stop. I run through the barricade and fall by the side of the road. Horváth: *It's time for the snow plow!* We look around to see if one is coming down the road. It is the sort of humour which spreads like an infection. I am soaking wet, shivering and exhausted.

55

There are special arrangements for New Year's Eve: a joint party with the students of the village *gymnasium*. We are to practise our German conversational skills. The gym is emptied of all except for chairs lined up along the walls. In front, where there is a stage, the record player (gramophone) will be hooked up to some speakers. I volunteer to be in charge of the records and the music. I have never danced before, so I will have something to do. I arrange the records we have in order: two fast ones, one slow. It is big band music: Benny Goodman, Harry James, Les Elgart and the like.

56

There is a certain awkwardness, a certain timidity at first. Then, as the two strange groups intermingle, through words and movement, there is a general ennui about the music. There are several Austrian boys and girls who complain to me and give me records, mostly singles, to play. Presley, Bo Diddley, Pat Boone, and others, whom I haven't heard before. "O my Papa", a big European hit, I have heard. I put on the Elvis Presley records and the whole room becomes a swaying mass of bodies. I am pleased; after all, I am the "disc jockey", the instrument of this pleasure. The girl who gave me the Presley records speaks English and introduces me to the name and functions of the "disc jockey". When I put on Bo Diddley's "Johnny Be Good", primitive chaos ensues. I am about to follow it up with Pat Boone's slow-paced "Love Letters in the Sand" when two fat Austrian girls show up chanting: *We love this fucking rock and roll. Let's have it again!* I understand the message, although *fucking* is not in my vocabulary. Horváth rushes in and sends me off to have a good time. Meanwhile he insists on taking over "disc jockeying", muttering

that things are getting out of control. I translate this for one of
the Austrian girls and she laughs: *Out of control? That is good!*
And we dance, out of control, to "Love Letters in the Sand". I
realize one does not "learn" to dance to this music, one just eases
into it.

57

A tall, attractive Hungarian girl is keen on me. She has been
encouraging, but so far I have done nothing about it. I ask her
for a dance and we have several. Then we step outside for fresh
air and a look at the skies. The warmth of her embrace and lips
makes me forget about the chill of the night. There is a problem:
our noses get in the way. We manage to overcome that. She is
from Eisenstadt, where the Eszterházys used to keep a castle.

58

In April I get a telegram from Mother: *Come immediately. We are
ready to leave for Canada.* I am heartbroken. I do not wish to
leave, but must. Attila, Balázs and my room-mates and I sneak
out of the dormitory through a window late at night. We go to
an *auberge*, order food and drink rum—Balázs insists it is the
only thing to drink. We drink to eternal friendship, no matter
where we all end up. Attila, in a gloomy mood, looks at the
ground and remarks that we all know where we will end up. All
of us. We walk back to school, hands linked in a chain, singing
Hungarian folk songs:

*Deres már a határ,
öszül a vén betyár. . .*

I vomit throughout the rest of the night while the others sleep
the sleep of the just. We never see each other again.

59

I am in a depressed daze for the rest of the Western European crossing. We meet in Vienna and then Mother, Edit and I travel by train to Salzburg to join a group destined for Canada. Surprise. I have been here before. Mother and I are walking along the embankment. Just at the end of the war, we were going to settle in the West—my father was aiming to reach the American zone, or what was to be the American zone. The Germans were retreating from the Russians. We were first stripped by German troops—car, food, clothing taken. Whatever was successfully hidden, or escaped their quick attention, was taken by the second troop of thieves—the Russians.

60

Salzburg was bombed, there were explosions. People were rushing to shelters, screaming, dying. Very little evidence is left of this along the embankment in the heart of the city. One huge crater created by a spectacular bomb stands unfilled. Perhaps a reminder. Why didn't we make it to the West in 1945? There was a group of Hungarians. It was a matter of crossing a river to what was to become West Germany. The women, my mother the most vociferous among them, insisted on going the very evening we arrived. But the men wanted to wait until the next day, expecting another group of Hungarians. When the morrow came, there was a group of unexpected Russian soldiers, shooting, stealing, raping. The Hungarians were all taken and declared to be prisoners of war. After this, the sight of the famous Salzburg Music Festival leaves little impression on me.

61

I picture the Russians searching my mother. She has already slipped some of her remaining jewelry into my sister Éva's shoe. Now she tells her to go for a walk in the meadow carrying her shoes in her hands. We live on the money from the jewels for two years.

62

We go on to Munich, then to Bremenhaven where we are to board a ship for the transatlantic voyage. As I look at the grey ocean in front of us, I am taken by its vast openness—it is inviting and full of mystery and possibilities. I look back at the cluttered land of Europe, old and wrinkled by thousands of years of suffering. I feel as if the layers of my past are peeling off. The ship is Greek; it is impeccably white and the crew is barbarously multilingual—they speak a bit of all languages. Babel: *Ok; jawol; d'accord; jól van; yeah!*

63

The ocean is one huge metallic sheet of grey. The cabin is miniscule. The bunk is narrow and hard. I am desperately seasick. After a day's fasting, I am told to go and eat. The dining room is large, cheerful, and there is a plethora of food. The ship's physician tells me to eat something light. I have soup and soft-boiled eggs. Then the dessert is produced for those sitting around me. A large plate of jello makes its appearance—it is green and slithery, slippery, it undulates with the waves like an organism with a life of its own. As I watch this strange edible thing, mesmerized, I have to rush out to the deck.

64

A day later I feel better. I explore the ship. There are movies to see, swimming to do, a library to read in. But for a few hours each afternoon, I stand in the drizzling rain on deck, watching the life of the sea and the ship. A week later we are pushing into the St. Lawrence, stopping at Quebec City briefly, and then: Montréal. At the last meal on the ship, I brave jello. This time it is purple. I close my eyes and take a spoonful to my tongue and swallow. Mother: *Anyone who can eat this stuff is either North American-born or is a North American no matter where he was born!*

# SOMETHING ELSE

1958–1966

# IN LIGHT OF CHAOS

"Don't apologize for anything, don't leave anything out; look and say what it's really like—but you must see something that throws new light on the facts."

–Wittgenstein

## 1

Montreal. Terra firma feels less than firm upon disembarking. It is as if the waves have pervaded my being. Éva and Gyuri are waiting for us. Customs and Immigration is a huge barn-like building devoid of a human face—the employees, mechanical and unsmiling, check baggage and documents. Identities established and fixed, we escape into the fresh air and freedom of Montreal which Gyuri describes as the Paris of North America. We cry for joy, reunited.

## 2

The apartment is just above a tavern at the corner of Decarie and Queen Mary. My room looks onto the street. It is late May and unusually hot and humid. The window must be kept open, but the noise of the traffic is tremendous. Huge trucks, mixing cement, grind to a halt at the traffic lights of the intersection, then start again. I try shutting the window. Now the noise subsides a little, but the heat is intolerable. I fall into an uneasy, fitful half-sleep, crossing the border, hearing explosions all around me. This is a nightly occurrence for the duration of our two-year stay in this flat.

## 3

I need to get a job for the summer. A Hungarian friend of Gyuri's works for Bell Telephone. Something might turn up there. The building is in the heart of downtown. I am led into the bowels of the building—downstairs where the cafeteria and the kitchen are. Here I am "interviewed" and given the job of dishwasher and general help for the summer. I am asked: Am I at least sixteen years old? I am short a few months but the friend of the family quickly answers for me: He just turned sixteen the other day. The interviewer is very attractive, impeccably cared for and seductively plump. Overwhelmed by desire and reduced to silence by the failure of being under the magic age of sixteen, I follow her into the busy and bustling kitchen. Here my duties are to dispose of the leftovers on the incoming plates and then pile them and arrange them for the steam dishwasher, a monster of ten feet in length; onto the assembly line of this monster go the arranged dishes for a thorough cleaning and steaming. She leaves us, hips swaying as she walks in beauty, gingerly moving through the chaos of the large kitchen, having thrown the staff—Greeks, Italians, a few French-Canadians and now a Hungarian—into a hypnotic trance: *That is a dish I want to clean and steam myself*—thus my Italian fellow worker and teacher of the strange ways of the culinary underworld.

4

A big plus of the job is free food; breakfast, snacks, lunches are gratis. While my fellow workers munch away heartily, I have nothing apart from a glass of apple juice and toast. The vast quantities of leftover food, in various stages of decay, undermine my appetite. I sit quietly during coffee break observing the hordes of incoming staff. Canadian chicken tastes like fish, I say. They deny it vehemently. A little later I find out that chickens are force-fed all sorts of things, sometimes fish. I am beginning to think I am unsuitable for North America—one needs nourishment to live and none of it, the indigenous stuff, do I find edible.

5

Glorious pay-day: Friday. On the way back from work I stop at Steinberg's, a local supermarket. On my first visit, the display of masses of food makes me nauseous. The contrast with what is available elsewhere induces a dissonance in me, as if I were responsible for what others can not have. These twinges of conscience subside after a while until I become immune to the sights and sounds of the marketplace. Now I just go for the ice cream: chocolatey, creamy, and I can eat it! This is my big reward each Friday—a quart of ice cream and a flick. With pride I surrender my salary to Mother.

6

Hitchcock's *Vertigo* is the week's other reward. I am totally absorbed: our administrative secretary, the hypnotic beauty, is stalking the silver screen in the form of Kim Novak. I feel a jolt and a sudden loss. The realization that the ambulating work of art, Miss Sikowsky, is a copy, a fake of a Hollywood actress, deflates me. I become suspicious of the surface, of appearances. I keep a vigil for authenticity, for originality. *L'homme, c'est le style lui-même.* I discuss the issue at home; Gyurka, of robust common sense, says: *Kim Novak is a fine model for personal looks if one happens to be a girl.* At work I whisper the secret to the Italian who desires to "clean and steam this porcelain dish"— she is not original; she is a Kim Novak copy. If you can't have the real thing, a good copy is good, he says. Another lover of wisdom joins in: How can anyone in his right mind seek originality in a country where Coke is the *real* thing? Such values are European imports—my youth and recent arrival explain my naïveté. As I bend over the plates, cleaning off the french fries and egg yolks and half-eaten sausages, I silently hold forth for authenticity. I like the remark of the old French-Canadian woman in charge of the steaming dishwasher: *L'homme, c'est le style.* Do I have a distinctive style? Is this something that happens to one as one lives or is it something acquired by deeds? A fog sets in. Is it the question or is it the steam of the dishwasher that has this effect?

7

It is a muggy, intolerably hot August weekend. I go to Ile St. Helene. The beach is packed with oiled, baked bodies. I swim quite far into the St. Lawrence and then, when I look up, I see in the distance a gigantic ocean liner heading into Montreal. I swim frantically back to shore and then watch through half-closed eyelids as it passes: a huge white structured blob on a greyish-green surface with the sand as foreground. My bit of mental painting is terminated by the ship's disgorging some of its rubbish into the river. This is an event I am unprepared for—no National Film Board work depicted this!

8

I comb the beach aimlessly. A brown-skinned, freckled girl, my age, in a black bikini, is building sandcastles. My efforts to be extra careful so as not to damage them backfire. One is knocked down and disintegrates into formless sand. She looks up and then stands in mock combat: *Maintenant, tu dois le reconstruire.* I confess that I do not understand what she is saying. *Ah, you are English,* she says in English in a melodious, soft way. *No, no, Hungarian, émigré.* She decides to teach me French right there and then. *Je suis Hongrois, et je m'appelle Béla. Elle s'appelle Claire.* She appears charmed by my guttural pronunciation. I love her ready smile and baptize her éclair: a bakery product I recently discovered. After these preliminaries, we dive into the river. Pretending to be a shark, I attack her under water, lift her up and then submerge again. She is delighted by the game and I am too. Under water I caress her breasts and feel the sudden inflation and gravity of my loins. She puts her hand on it gently and then pinches it, laughing, then breaks away, giving me a wet kiss. Her parents are calling—time to go home. She shouts her number—Hunter four and something. I want to rush out and confirm it. But, embarrassed by my erection, I stay in the water and swim it off. Subsequently I try variations of the number I think she gave me. Wrong number, I am told. Impressions of her body, *joie de vivre,* her airs of innocence and guilty camaraderie are almost as tangible elements of my first Montreal summer as the hot dishes I occasionally drop as they come off the "steam machine".

9

The time for school registration arrives. There are several schools
in the area: West Hill High; it won't take me. Am I a Catholic or
a Protestant? Well, this is a Protestant school. Gyurka dispenses
advice: *Go to Selwyn House in Westmount, a very fine school—
private, perhaps they wish to enrich their school by a student with
a "différence".* I take the bus along Sherbrooke and get off just
before Greene. The registrar exudes suspicion and contempt.
This is not a school for immigrants; even if it were, the annual
fee is an unaffordable sum for me. And even if I could afford it,
they are full—no more students. No attempt to discuss my past
achievements. This man is indifferent to whether I live or die! I
feel. The limits of freedom found are sharply drawn. As I walk
out, dazed by his arrogant nonchalance, it dawns on me: freedom is not enough.

10

I walk up Sherbrooke, west. Depressed. I find Daniel O'Connell
High School—small, modest and somewhat neglected. The principal is a Dominican monk. His habit, black and long, is in need
of cleaning. He has a brush-cut, is tall and gaunt and there is
warmth in his eyes. He asks me for my last report card. He puts
me in "third year high" and excuses me from French for half a
semester. School uniform: jacket and tie of any description will
suffice. Subjects: Latin grammar, Latin texts, mathematics, history, English grammar and literature, chemistry, physics. In the
second term I am to add French grammar and literature. His
logic: one language at a time. My vocabulary does not seem to
impress him—but there is an unmistakable sense of welcome.
*May you fare well in your studies with us,* he says. He forgot to
mention religious studies.

11

There is no instruction in class in the sense of the teacher covering, explaining and discussing the subject matter. We are given assignments in class and then, if there are difficulties, they are supposed to be addressed. To begin with this feels strange to me. There is no stimulus, in my experience provided by the teacher, to fall in love with the subject. Hence, I pay the closest attention to the subject itself. While it feels lonely with the text, every now and then I am rewarded by a sense of discovery, of insight, without a guide or intermediary. One of my favourite subjects is Latin texts; Brother Bernard, red-faced, ruddy-nosed, uncommunicative, in his early sixties, sits at his desk and assigns us *The Conquest of Gaul.* I struggle with the translation, and finally come up with an interesting piece. There is a controversy about the correct rendering. Brother Bernard will adjudicate, his gaze directed downwards towards his habit. Then the sound of a book falling and those of us sitting in front see a copy of *Coles Notes* for Latin texts, and Brother Bernard, embarrassed and sheepish, tries to recover the "forbidden aid". I am now skeptical about Brother Bernard's adjudicating powers concerning the best translation. I decide to avail myself of a copy of *Coles Notes*, the last tribunal, the privileged reading—all for one dollar. Soon I become skeptical about the reliability of *Coles* too, for some of the difficult passages give difficulties to whoever did the *Coles* translations. I feel strangely relieved and my enthusiasm for the Roman historians is greater than ever.

12

Mr. Rioux does English and French with us. He is big on memorization. Hence I memorize "To Lucasta, on Going to the Wars"—being especially keen on the line "I would not love thee dear so much / Would I not love Honour more." I notice with satisfaction that the anonymous poet is also fond of it, for he repeats it often. "Shall I compare thee to a Summer's Day?" and other sonnets of Shakespeare pass our lips, as one by one we are asked to recite it. If someone falters, some helpful catalytic whisper from the adjacent seat usually works. No one can memorize Francis Thompson's "The Hound of Heaven", for it is too long. Instead, we discuss it. The metaphor running through the poem—God, the persistent hound, our soul, the quarry. Sullivan, sitting in front of me, complains loudly about there never being a dog-catcher around when one needs one. Rioux: *I heard that, Sullivan. Please report to the Principal's office.* Rioux himself is fond of a good overture; he starts a brief talk on sex education by saying: *I know you guys, you get an erection by just looking at a light bulb.* The difference between our secular and sacred teachers. . .

13

This is an all-boys school. The mix: the students come mostly from lower Notre Dame de Grâce, most of them Irish and Italian. There is another Hungarian boy—he is a source of amazement. He knows exactly what he wants in life: to be an engineer. He will join the armed forces as a cadet, then go on to McGill to do engineering. At lunch he plays checkers while I eat dry sandwiches, reading Raymond Chandler's *The Big Sleep* and *The Long Goodbye.* If I want to be anything at all, then I want to be Phil Marlowe, private eye, aiding the victims, unpuzzling the crime, a friend of the downtrodden, a comforter of beautiful but misguided women. The idea of wanting to be something, of choosing a profession, disturbs me, limits me. I find it repugnant. I don't want to be boxed in.

14

Religious studies: chiefly the history of the Church, hence a lot of medieval history. I am astounded by the elaborate and lucid explanations for obscure and seemingly impossible dogmas, doctrines, *ex cathedra* pronouncements. The history is interesting and far from dark: the Church as the motor of history. Do I believe these things? I don't know what they mean, how to settle truth or falsehood here. They are like knots at the end of a string—if you don't have them, things unravel. But things unravel in any event.

15

There are words which are different, yet I pronounce them the same. "And" and "end" is one such pair. I watch the CBC news, attending carefully to the announcer's pronunciation. On the weekends I tune in for a film with Bogart and Bacall, adapted for the screen from Raymond Chandler's book. I imagine the scenes, the characters, rather differently. The film is impoverished when compared to my reading of the book. Yet it has a life of its own and I enjoy it.

16

Saturday morning Mother makes crêpes Suzette, or, alternately, doughnuts. Gyurka and I sit at the table facing one another in mock-competition. He wins—he eats fifteen doughnuts to my twelve. A new record!

17

Éva and Gyurka are getting married. The ceremony is at the old Hungarian Catholic Church on St. Lawrence. I am given a brown suit for the occasion and a brush cut. The top of my head is really bristling: I pass my palm over it often; it gives a tickling sensation resulting in a strange shiver along my spine. They are off for a honeymoon to the Laurentians, to St. Donat. I am happy, for Éva looks so happy. When the three of us, Mother, Edit and I, return to the apartment, I feel as if truncated, as if some bodily part were missing.

18

I explore the city on foot, revelling in the loneliness of the long-distance walker. On walking back from the mountain I become famished. I stop at a Chicken Chalet and ask what I can have for thirty cents. French fries. She directs me to the take-out service in the back. Here I get a big paper bag of french fries, steaming hot, made from potatoes cut on the premises, and golden brown. Next to ice cream, this becomes a central feature of my staple on Saturdays.

19

Sitting on a bench eating french fries, in the park at Girouard and Sherbrooke West, I see some boys playing soccer. One of the boys is from my school, Andrew Gattuso. It is an all-Italian affair. They scream, demanding the ball; only the swearing and the obscenities are spoken in English or French, with th2 occasional *Disgraziata* interjected. I wave at Gattuso; he is stocky and22as a permanent limp, although a slight one. He comes over and asks if I would like to play. So I do; for an hour and a half I play right wing and score two goals. *Madrid has Puskás; we Spartakos have Béla Ungarese!* says Gattuso. As we walk triumphantly to celebrate our victory, playing pin-ball and having soft drinks, insults are hurled at us from windows: *Mon Dieu Wops, get back across the tracks you fucking Wops!* Gattuso says happily: *Deep down they really love us. Without us their life would be so boring. And they would have to work harder too. Who would build their buildings without us?* Gattuso's father is in the construction business.

20

Winter arrives and drags on. It just won't go away, taking more months out of the year than I am accustomed to. I study, read, watch films on TV and hibernate. I come across the writings of Dashiell Hammett. What a find! Sam Spade I add to my list of heroes. In spite of this, I am beginning to feel as if I am trapped and can't get out.

21

Mother cleans house and looks after two children whose parents are both working. She takes the bus at eight each morning and returns at five. Edit works as a waitress and studies English. Éva is a draftsman at an architectural firm. Gyurka is with a firm of chartered accountants and at night he attends Sir George Williams College taking courses leading to a Bachelor of Commerce. Late one night, there is a call. Gyurka and I rush downtown to the Carmen Café—a Hungarian café where Edit works. She had an epileptic attack. Her tongue is doubled in size and badly chewed. No one had the presence of mind or sufficient knowledge to put a hand in her mouth to prevent this. We take her to a hospital and then home. She is given pills, to be taken daily, which suppress the tendency to attacks of *petit mal*. Once the silence of the night resumes, I have a crisis of conscience: Why should Edit work rather than me? Why shouldn't she go to school? I have a feeling of immense guilt. Finally I fall into a fitful sleep. As I am crossing the border again, for the nth time, I dream that I can not escape—there is no exit. The milieu is different, but everything else is the same. I wake up to the sound of a cement-mixer truck grinding to a halt at the intersection. The winter blanket of snow makes these sounds and noises somewhat muffled. I open the door and let the chill penetrate the room. I resolve to be single-minded and practical, to take care and provide for my people here. Being a dollar short of the required taxi fare, as we brought Edit back, brings on the image of the exploited black on the streets of New York—in rags, dishevelled, sick, starving. A fact of life that was the focus of Communist propaganda. Except that now the image is enriched. We immigrants are there with the black man, frozen in misery.

I take deep breaths, pound my chest like a gorilla about to attack, and commit myself to *success* through *work.*

22

Mother asks, *Do you remember, gypsies at the village fair?* A wild, wrinkled, long-haired woman passing her hands over my body, looking at my hands, tracing something or other, perhaps nothing. She looks up startled, thereby startling me, and cackles to Mother: *You have a good one here; he will become a great man, but lots of pain.* Suddenly she grabs me, hugs me and whispers in my ear: *There is nothing to fear.* Mother, amused, gives her the twenty forints and complains: *So what's new? They all grow up and everywhere is pain.* I do remember this incident. But when I mention my twinges of conscience about going to school while everyone else is working and making money, she brings up the episode, perhaps to set me a goal.

23

I am promoted to fourth-year high without writing finals. First in class with an eighty-five average. Brother Bernard is full of praise: *Look, an immigrant boy who to begin with hardly speaks English leads the class. You better improve your study habits. The outside world is harsh; it will chew you up and spit you out unless you are vigilant!* I wish Brother Bernard would not say this for my classmates are visibly irked by comparisons of this sort. All except Gattuso.

24

Gattuso is utterly indifferent to scholastic achievement. While Brother Bernard, somewhat hard of hearing, shouts his comments on report cards, Gattuso is passing around a note. It is a photo of a fat, hairy, naked woman, seated on a chair and masturbating. The note says: Diverse poses are available, fifty cents each. I pass this on after due inspection. Brother Bernard becomes aware of a certain lack of attention to his comments. In an agile manner, hitherto unobserved, he pounces upon the photo and the note and seizes them. He looks at them and goes into an apoplexy, a paroxysm. Then he calls Gattuso, mispronouncing his name: Get-oozo, Get-oozo. He grabs Gattuso's ears and leads him to the Principal's office. We speculate on the punishments that will be allotted. How is a student to be punished at the end of a school year? Perhaps they will withhold his report card. But Gattuso would welcome that. Then we hear the sounds of strapping and the screams of Gattuso. We count twenty straps—a form of punishment reserved for *gross* misconduct.

25

The marks are posted, not in alphabetical order, but in order of achievement and standing. Nothing is hidden but the privacy of the confessional.

26

Back in the bowels of the Bell Telephone building—Beaver Hall. At the entrance there are beavers in bas-relief decorating the walls. I have never seen a real beaver. They look much like squirrels except bigger and fatter. Gyuri instructs: the maple tree and the beaver are symbols of Canada because of their prevalence. Maple syrup is to be used on pancakes and I should be an eager beaver at washing dishes for the month of July.

27

Only the two ancient French-Canadian women in charge of the steam monster and the Kim Novak look-alike administrative secretary appear to be permanent fixtures at the cafeteria. Things have to change in order to stay the same; a new lot of immigrants have taken the place of the former lot. Our relationship to Kim

Novak is altered: while ostensibly she is the object of our desire, I realize that there is theatre enacted here. The whistles, the appreciative comments are part of the Italian workers' social repertoire, and Kim's strutting about is simply her doing her thing. It is no longer charged with energy or vitality. Well, perhaps it's me. Perhaps the magic of novelty is gone.

28

Our soccer team loses against a Montreal-Greek team. The Greeks are generally older and stronger; they play very rough. Whenever one of us gets hurt, their supporters cheer. We are further demoralized when we hear the referee speak Greek to the captain of the opposing team. We lodge a complaint against the referee with the soccer association. Our horrible thought: they do not merely want to win, like us. They want to hurt us.

29

Music and dancing at St. Anne de Bellevue, on the outskirts of Montreal. Our local Italian connection tells us that there is a live band and the girls are *fantastico*. The night club is a large barn; there are lots of girls, some unaccompanied. I sense a certain unease, a tension amongst the locals as I look around. After a little while we start dancing. I dance with a thin, terribly sad-looking unaccompanied girl. We speak little; she speaks French: *Je suis Béla; je m'appelle Michelle. Enchanté. Tu danses bien, merci.* Both of us nervous, we clutch at each other somewhat desperately. The number ends and I return to our table. My team-mates are adventurous. They are dancing with some incredibly attractive girls whose boyfriends watch in a state of frozen fury. The band takes a break. Suddenly a flood of forty or fifty French-Canadian boys are hitting and slapping us, moving us towards the exit, swearing, screaming. The huge doorman joins in the action, against us, of course. The fight is short-lived. We are badly outnumbered. Our faces black and blue, doubled

over in pain, we get into the car and start heading back to
Montreal. My Italian friends are recounting their adventures with
the girls and plotting a vendetta. I am in pain, pensive and quiet.
Have I escaped and crossed the Atlantic to be stabbed by some
jealous French-Canadian boy trying to protect his girlfriend
against the advances of the macho Italians? From now on soccer,
books and friendly gatherings for me. No violence, no thanks.

30

My very first vacation. We set out for Brome Lake in the Eastern
Townships. Gyuri drives us in a large rented car. Montreal feels
like a steam bath; as we drive, the air becomes less oppressive
and there is a sense of relief, much like being let out of a house
after being cooped up for several weeks. There are small farms
with wonderful houses on them. My vision is unencumbered by
tall buildings or hills or mountains. The landscape is in open view
and I hungrily take in the fields, trees, sky and, of course, french
fries from the vendors at the stops we make. I individuate and
dwell on the items of the storehouse of nature; I walk on all fours
and roll in the grass like a dog. The pleasurable life.

31

I resolve to follow nature and get up with the sun. The lake is
absolutely calm, like glass. In a row-boat I cut away from the
shore and cast the line. The catch is promising, numerous if
small. Needing to relieve myself, I land on strange shores. It is
wildly overgrown. I feel as if some of the leaves are carnivorous,
about to take a bite out of me. On my return, I clean the fish and
fry them for breakfast. It is wonderful. Soon after I acquire an
almost unrelievable itch. Yearning for relief, I plunge into the
cool waters of the lake. No end to itching. I am told that this is
an affair of poison ivy. Whisked to the small hospital at Cowans-
ville, I am given medication and a soothing, creamy lotion to be
applied to the skin three times a day. The book of nature can not

be read just like that: it is not an open book. Those clandestine,
surreptitious green leaves temper somewhat my brief love affair
with nature.

32

007 enters and saves two days of otherwise insufferably conscious itching. Gyurka and I take turns at Ian Fleming's James
Bond adventures at espionage. *On Her Majesty's Secret Service*
and *Dr. No* I polish off voraciously. Subsequently, the world of
objects and persons acquires an added dimension for me. People
and things have a depth—they are not to be judged on the basis
of mere surface or appearance. This happy, casual American
family, frolicking and playing on the beach, may in fact be from
Vermont, as they say. But perhaps they work for the CIA, KGB
or S.M.E.R.S.H. I have fun by engineering different scenarios. It
dawns on me: my world and their world can not be read off me
or them just like that either. Conversation helps—so I immediately approach the best-looking daughter. I have tried talking to
the lake, but received no response. The girl from Vermont does
respond, however. We go to the *auberge* at night, eat hot dogs
and dance. Then she announces to her parents that we are going
for a walk. On the deserted beach we lie in the sand, gripping
one another; then dive into the water to cool off. We are leaving
the next day, back to Montreal, back to school.

33

There is a fire in the chemistry laboratory. Its cause is a mystery.
I suggest that it is spontaneous combustion, a concept we
acquired recently but could find no use for. The explanation is
widely adopted, especially among the smokers. I play and amuse
myself by inventing roles for otherwise idle concepts—yet some
take it seriously. Even Brother Dominic, the principal, adopts it
in his report to the School Board. But only as a last resort, since
his investigation could not determine the cause of the fire.

34

There is a queue for the confessional box. There is a wonderful silence in the church—disturbed only by the occasional chatter of girls from our sister school, or crude exchanges between boys in the queue and the absolved exiting the confessional: Hey, so how many times did you jerk off in the past two weeks?

35

I confess: to the occasional misdeed, to the suddenly discerned nasty thought, to the intermittent overwhelming prick of desire. In the patience of that silence, of that expectant, voraciously hungry capacity to listen and to forgive, having run out of sins I invent a more interesting case for myself, against myself. I sigh with relief at the *Absolvo te in nomine patri. . .* and rush out of the prison of the box, innocence and freedom regained, for the moment, yet hitherto never lost. The pretense at self-reflection is like being buried alive in a coffin.

36

The Latin grammar text's title charms me: *Living Latin,* it calls the dead language. For me, its study is not like medical pathology— you learn your English and French grammar through Latin, we are told in the justificatory moods of our teacher. For me Latin, both grammar and Roman historical texts, is as lively as a beehive. The dicta, the proverbs, the epigrams, one of which heads each chapter, gives a certain direction, paves a road, offers instruction and counsel for life. What the counsel actually means, how I am to use it, engages me. *Carpe diem*: the translation given is "Pluck the day's opportunities." I prefer my own "Seize the day." But how does this translate into life? Am I to act on any passion that occurs? Conjugations, declensions give me a frame-work of discipline. Having no goals, not knowing what I am to do, confronted with constant flux, I escape into the edifice of my studies.

37

In Quebec the Ministry of Education sets the final examinations. I graduate with the highest honours in the College Preparatory Course, being among the top ten students in the province. Devoid of a sense of achievement, having no idea as to what to do, no one volunteering advice, I fall back on solid ground: I must work and help pay bills—buy food and do my share in the family, then attend college at night at Sir George Williams. This is a "worker's university", as well as for drop-outs who have come to see the way. I wonder what I will be doing there, neither a worker nor a drop-out, nor do I see the way.

38

Five of us graduands decide to celebrate having survived high school and the ritualized Church celebrations arranged for graduation. Gattuso knows just the place; it is near Dorchester and rue Guy. Dim lights, loud, noisy music, a makeshift stage and a dazed clientele. We try to look older by acting as if we were *des hommes du monde*. I decide to have a cognac. For a small fortune, I get something that tastes awful—odious. Gattuso whispers: *Order a beer—we are here for the show*. Suddenly the makeshift stage is lit and a woman of Amazonian proportions appears; hips swaying, eyes rolling, she proceeds to strip off her scant wardrobe. As I watch, it strikes me as if this were a lesson in the anatomy of the incongruous Amazon. The huge upper torso, the cylindrical thighs and the rouged face writhe in an awkward, clumsy way. *An amateur*, says Gattuso. I am beginning to feel nauseous. What passes for cognac does me in. I can't wait for the "pro"—grab a cab and am homebound.

## 39

As I am crossing the border, one of the ghostly watchtowers comes to life. I hear a voice—a command to stop. I look back but keep on walking. A face is lit up and I am startled: it is Dr. Budai, about to shoot—he shoots. I recognize myself sliced in half, vertically, and I fall to the ground. I wake up on the floor, having fallen out of bed, screaming for help, but all there is, is the stench of cognac and drops of sweat.

## 40

Mother baby-sits and cleans house for the Gottliebs, our Hungarian friends. Erika is a librarian at Sir George and Pali is in advertising, at night doing his Master's in literature. Erika's father, Dr. Simon, is the chief chemist at the Sherwin-Williams Paint factory in Verdun. I have a job, at the bottom of the ladder, where I can look up and try to do my best. The job: cleaning test-tubes and washing equipment in the research lab.

## 41

Pigments cloud the air. Infernal deep tanks, full of paint, the grind of dry materials and then the wet sound of mixing, workers rolling huge drums. Technicians in white lab coats take samples. Then the quieter labs where the research is done. I am given a white lab coat and plastic gloves, positioned above a large sink filled with xylene, and set to clean beakers, test tubes and diverse equipment involved in experimental work. The odour of xylene, a milder-than-turpentine odour, pervades my clothes, my skin, my whole being. For what seems like eternity, I seem to be composed of xylene.

## 42

Sir George Williams is housed in a building on Drummond near St. Catherine. It is connected physically and historically to the

YMCA. At night it is bustling with the business of educating the serious and the mature. Seriousness and gravity are sculpted on the faces I see. People of all ages go about the business of learning. There is anonymity, long corridors and large introductory classes. Lectures are solemn, uninterrupted by questions or discussion. All trim meat, no fat. My history professor says: *If I meet you in the corridor and you say "hello" and I ignore you, please do not take this personally. I just don't remember you.* Everyone takes notes frantically. I refuse to do any such thing.

43

At five-thirty I float onto the bus, feather-light and exuding chemical fumes. The fumes are sharp and pungent; even on a crowded bus, fellow passengers try to avoid my proximity. I hear: I hate the odour of xylene, when in fact one girl greets another: How are you Ilene? Solo, I sit in the upper left-hand corner of the lecture theatre, fuming. My identity with xylene seems firmly established, unshakable. I mourn my fate and grumble: why couldn't I be lucky and be some organic pre-Socratic compound like water, earth or fire? But then again, it could be worse.

44

Éva is pregnant. She and Gyurka get their own place and Mother, Edit and I move into an apartment near Girouard and Côte St. Luc. I have a quiet room overlooking the gardens of nearby duplexes. Finally, fresh air and only a faint murmur of traffic. As I enter the room, I am aware of a visitor. A small, black, winged rodent-like creature, confused by the light, circles around. Taken aback, I get a broom and resolve to rid myself of this rabies-carrier, this radar-equipped rodent. On the third try I manage to bat it through the window—it flies happily into the night. Where I was born, in Kolozsvár, Transylvania, there were clouds of bats on summer evenings, blackening the sky. So Mother tells me.

And now a French-Canadian bat's visit. I firmly draw the limits of Transylvanian solidarity.

45

Gyurka changes his name from "Mihalcsics" to "Michaels". Pronouncing "Mihalcsics" puts unprecedented linguistic demands on the inflexible tongues of Montreal's Anglo-Saxon community. By singling him out, it distracts from the business of the chartered accountant. It would hinder him in the long march upward through business institutions. You pay a certain sum of money, and you are reborn under a new name. The pragmatics of secular baptism.

46

Dark and olive-skinned, my boss called Spiro takes me aside: *Béla, I hear you go to night school immediately after work. Well, pack it in half an hour earlier and take a shower before going to school.* The showers are just next door. There is an incessant flow of test tubes, vials and beakers coming in. At four o'clock, I leave them, with the official blessing and a few twinges of conscience. Tomorrow is another day. What amazes me even more than his counsel is that Spiro pronounces my name correctly.

47

Cleansed and purified, with a hint of a pleasant aftershave, I catapult myself into the bus. I transfer at Atwater. The bus is packed like a can of sardines. Body pressed against bodies, feeling the breaths that are taken, the sighs that are released; no longer aware of my own exuded odours, I become sharply aware of those exuded by others. Our arms clutching the bar above, armpits are exposed; wet, natural or deodorized, stench blends with colognes or perfumes. As the driver suddenly brakes, I feel pressing against me, against my back, flesh that has a life of its own—heaving breasts, pulsating nipples. Before I can turn my head, we are tossed in reverse, my nose in the malodorous armpit of someone tall, hard-hatted. As I get off, a fresh breeze blows.

### 48

It is Friday. Amid the discarded cans of paint and chemicals, against the stained-white lab coats of technicians, comes dancing, elegant, fragrant, as if from another world, Spiro's secretary, Mademoiselle Meunier, distributing the pay cheques. "Bella," she calls me. I am too anxious to inhale her, to have her through these vibrating olfactory sensations she produces in this factory of paints; so I resist saying: *Mademoiselle, vous êtes "bella"; je m'appelle "Béla".* Last night on the late show I saw a Dracula movie with "Bella" Lugosi. He is so pale and sad. Oh, my long-lost uncle Bella, he made it big in Hollywood, after his death. Another uncle of mine, "Bella" Bartók, also made it big in New York, after his death. Perhaps *les Américains* like their Hungarians dead—and then they recognize them. Thus me, smiling as slyly as I can. Mademoiselle Meunier hums cleverly: *But Bella, I recognize you and you're very much alive.*

### 49

First-year college, leading to the Bachelor of Science degree: it takes me a year and a half, including summer courses, to complete first year. Introductory English is a compulsory course: I can either do English as a second language, or the course for native speakers. I choose the second option. The instructor is a broad-faced, suited grammatical terrorist. We write reports on assigned topics, reveal our sources and references, footnote and compile bibliography. He assigns sections of our text, *Writing With a Purpose*, for home study. Then he tests us on these sections. I write book reviews, reports, essays. He pores through each with a zeal and meticulousness that generate in me a mixture of odium and admiration. Language freezes in his hands; stiff and brittle, it does not invite employment but discourages it. He teaches English as if it were a dead language. This inspires me. I pretend that the essence of English is to be grasped, right there and then, from *Writing With a Purpose.* I pretend to be a pathologist looking at the organs of a corpse with detachment. But then outside the class, and even inside, the corpse comes alive and moves with such cadence and fluidity, twists and turns, even as we speak. As it turns out, I am best at writing without a purpose. The terrorist of grammar gives me high marks for a "stream of consciousness" essay, an impromptu effort written in class.

50

The terrorist gives one A, two B's, three C's, a few D's and fails fifty percent of the class. I get a C. He is most conscientious, yet devastating; he succeeds in guarding a corpse that is beginning to rot. He almost triumphs in deterring lovers and mourners of language from paying respects to the corpse. But there is nothing like a grammatical terrorist to bring out the passion for the green valleys, the icy peaks and the rich and fertile plains of a living language. I pass English 100. Now I can fuck up the language as much as I please. For days I celebrate the anarchy of language. Alas, this is only a ritual. In practice, I begin to correct others and myself.

51

I run into Gattuso. He does first-year engineering at Sir George and skips lectures a lot, not liking any of it. He invites me to a party for someone who is getting married. Food, fiesta and entertainment. There is a price tag of seven dollars. The bridegroom is a distant cousin. Five of us from the old soccer team pile into a car, drive to a dilapidated small hotel in white shirts, suits and ties. I drink Martinis and eat mountains of spaghetti. The suite is packed with about fifty men ranging from twenty to forty in age. There are appreciative whistles and catcalls: two women, all legs, breasts and coiffured hair, enter. One, my age, is in black lingerie—stockings, garter belt and laced bikini; the other is a black girl similarly unattired. The one with red hair has a fight with the other girl: I want him, I dream about him! The other answers: No, you can't have him, he's all mine! They start wrestling—a mock fight over someone. Everyone eagerly forms a circle around them. Enter the bridegroom, fully tuxedoed, watching this fight, which has become quite physical, with increasing appetite. I am on the outer circles. Abandoning my plate of pasta, I move closer and see the two girls slapping, wrestling and tearing at each other. The groom authoritatively orders them to stop. They scream and attack him—tearing all his clothes off. The redhead tries to mount him while the black girl nibbles at his chest, trying to shove the other off. He finally asserts himself—he shoves one aside and has intercourse with the other. Then he, titillated by the neglected girl, marshals himself and enters her to the groans and moans of the girls and the hurrahs and encouragements of the crowd. Gattuso slaps me on the shoulders: *Stag party. The spaghetti is good but this is better,* he says. Overwhelmed by disgust and desire, I leave all this, seeking a more elusive good.

52

I am crawling flat on my stomach across the border. Mines explode, people wail and cry. Then a searchlight illuminates a field packed with wounded, cripples and nude bodies. Some pray, some are dead. A voice takes attendance—it comes from a watchtower: *Barbieri, Carver, Cunningham, de Tomasi, Findley, Spiro, Sullivan, Zabaidos, Wall.* . . Each of the announced responds and then—ten years' penance, thirteen years' purgatory. When it comes to Zabaidos, no one responds: twenty years of xylene in the labs of Sherwin-Williams. How can I be sentenced when I was not even called? You fake, you plastic, I say, you can't be what you pretend to be, you don't even know my name. *Unum nomen, unum nominatum!* Then the field of corpses joins me in chorus, to the tune of Verdi's "Nabucco", *Unum nomen, unum nominatum.* A cool reply: *How can I know your name when you haven't taught me to pronounce it?*

### 53

Next day I am promoted: I am now a technician in Quality Control, located in the central factory. The lab is small, space enough for three; it has lots of windows, light. Diametrically opposite to the windows, the door leading into the factory. There are five large tanks, mixing a hundred and fifty gallons of different paints. At specified stages of production, I take a sample and brush it on a small, square-shaped piece of treated gyproc. Then I compare it to the standardized colour chart for the product in question. The matching of colours is conducted under as constant light conditions as possible. It is not a mechanical procedure, for the very same quantities of ingredients—pigments, oils, thinners and what not—sometimes give different shades. The pigments may have different concentrations, or the tanks may have had residues of colours from the previous mix. Matching the standard on my own becomes a crowning achievement. I rush out to the blue overalled workers with my gyprocs, joyously muttering: we are getting close, just a touch of blue, or, just a touch of red. Sometimes it looks like a mismatch when wet. Patience, the foreman says; it is going to be close when dry. *D'accord.*

### 54

I sign up for organic chemistry and for physical chemistry. The lab period for organic chemistry is eight hours per week; physical chemistry has no lab, for the theory and the lab each constitute a full course. To begin with I just do the theory. Madras, the professor of chemistry, teaches this course. His lectures are marked by such clarity and lucidity that I am transported into a realm of standard colours—every sample matches the standard—no mismatches. Inspired, I fight against exhaustion, against the fatigue of my midnight shift, from midnight to eight in the morning, against the tedium, the monotony of the organic chemistry lab at nights. Sun, day, light cease to exist. I am engulfed in the black night of the blind elements of the Mendeleyev Periodic Table.

55

Up from Drummond, close to the college, there is a hamburger joint—A&W Root Beer, and indeed the Bear is there seated on the lap of a plump debutante drinking root beer. I have a quick snack and intend to browse in the little Classics bookshop close by. But the conviviality, the carefree atmosphere of the place, is magnetic. This is a hangout for the Sir George day students. I eagerly catch snippets of what sounds like an intellectual discussion. Imaginatively, I try to reconstruct it. But there are too many possible constructions. Which is the real one? Gloomy, I make towards the door, only to slip on some abandoned french fries; tumbling to the floor, I hear: *Now that is a real slip, a literal use of language, unlike a slip of the tongue, clearly a figure of speech.* Humiliated by a french fry I go away.

56

Dr. Simon, the Einstein of paint research and technology, walks the long corridors of the factory absorbed in thought. He is my mentor, but when we meet and I say "hello" he simply nods, unless he is lost in thought. His long, grey hair is like the mane of a horse, caught by the draft created by the many corridors and doors opening and shutting. He has invented a fire-resistant paint, but there is a small residual problem: brushability. It is hard to brush and apply. He brings a sample into Quality Control. When I brush it, I get the feeling of lifting weights. Disgruntled, he returns to his lab. *Coming up with fire-resistant paint is like looking for the* elixir vitae*!* says the fellow Quality Controller, when Dr. Simon is out of earshot. Quality Control is not noted for its faculty of imagination.

57

Occasionally I baby-sit Katika, when Éva and Gyurka go out on the rare Saturday. Katika asleep, I listen to music. Usually an opera and then mellow the harshness with some jazz. Gounod's *Faust*, with Nicholas Gedda, Victoria de Los Angeles and Boris Kristoff is now my favourite. Why would Faust transact such an incongruous trade? Why would he bargain his vitality, his spontaneity, for the mechanical, cyclical tedium of an eternal life? It is like being the great survivor, surrounded by a sea of death, aging, pain, yet being immune to it. Can one remain human under such conditions? I mellow out, dispelling such thoughts with the soothing sounds of Jack Teagarden and his trombone with his Dixieland-style band:

I've been just like a weary river
that keeps winding, the sweet,
Fate has been a very careful giver
to most everyone but me.
Oh how long it took me to learn
hope is strong, but tide after tide. . .
Every weary river meets the sea

58

The great tanks of paint are built into the ground, covered by lids; there is the constant grind of the mixing blades. If I close the lab door, it is a volcanic rumble. I step out to take a sample. It is about four in the morning. As I look at it, I see bits of hair, flesh and bone floating on top. Rushing to the control wall, pushing buttons, I stop the mixing and the stirring, screaming: *Tremblay, Tremblay, where are you?* The worker, a night-shift mate and humourist, mix-master of Sherwin-Williams, is nowhere to be seen. Searching the floor, haunted by images of Tremblay falling into the chasm of the paint tank, holding to the blade, revolving, and then ground! No Tremblay. Doubled over by a sudden stomach ache, I return to the lab about to telephone "emergency". I inspect the sample closely, mix it and find a small rodent's head, the eyes luminescent green with paint staring at me. Then the door opens and shuts: *Mon Dieu, qu'est-ce qui se passe? There are drops of paint everywhere! Bella, are you the sloppy bastard?* This is a "bella" moment indeed. I have never been so happy to hear my name mispronounced!

## 59

I no longer notice the difference between day and night. Indifferent and zombie-like, mechanically I carry out routines of the job, of school. The dark nights of despair are rarely lit, mostly during Madras's lectures in physical chemistry. Little Classics provides the literature to match my dominant mood: I go underground and exchange notes with Dostoyevsky. I feel as if I am stranger than Camus's *L'Étranger.* I walk the deserted roads of freedom with Sartre's Roguentin: a paralysis of will, an impression of the impotence of reason in spite of having reached the age of reason. I am a walking *Angst,* but where am I walking to? My routine deflates these imprecise concerns, but they return with a certain intolerable stubbornness. If the literature of *Angst* did not exist, I would have had to invent it, I begin to feel.

## 60

Gyurka graduates; he is a bachelor and yet he is married to my sister . . . no contradiction there. A Bachelor of Commerce. He is accepted to Harvard Business School to do graduate work in

Administration. *Would you go, Béla?* he asks. I say I would. He does not go. He decides to read for the Chartered Accountancy examinations to be held at McGill a year hence. Gyurka has character. He is solid and reliable. Comparing myself with him, I feel inadequate, like a man without qualities.

61

Yearning for substance, for qualities, I take on Qualitative Analysis: the course that strikes fear into the heart of chemistry majors and honours students. Seemingly interminable labs, from one lab to another. The white lab coat is no longer something I can take off and put on. Unwanted, yet it is as close as my skin. Utterly filthy, I surrender it to the cleaners, but it is born again, spotlessly institutionalized and handed to me by the supplies manager.

62

Sleepless and on the point of collapse, I withdraw from Quantitative and Qualitative Analysis. I admit defeat. Time opens its doors and welcomes me. My pets are Penguins in their classic editions; sources of solace and conversation: the soul talking with itself. I talk to myself, without moving my lips. And then talking to Penguins. I am as proud as Dr. Doolittle but for the fact that my pets and I reverse roles: they begin to feed me rather than me feeding them.

63

Promoted again: to paint formulator. I apprentice for two months and then am given a project to formulate a block sealer. For weeks I research various formulas for block sealers and make a small batch of each. Then I investigate samples of our competitors' block sealers. Does it yellow? Does it crack? Is it durable? Does it resist harsh climatic conditions? I test them and write up a report. Then, determining what ingredients are responsible for what qualities, I formulate a sealer that will supersede them all.

The first large batch is being made. I am wanted in the factory. There are difficulties—its viscosity is so low that it is burning the motors of the mixing blades. A larger quantity of solvent is needed to make its manufacture "operationally practical". I make the adjustment; the workers are happy, the motors hum and the product is now not much better than its competitors. Whittaker, the research lab supervisor, gentle, ash-grey hair, always encouraging: *Well, now we have a good block sealer; perfection is beyond our reach*. I am shattered. A sense of failure creeps in.

64

Whittaker: *Béla, here is a copy of Cronin's* The Citadel; *the making of a physician. With your kind of dedication, you might want to enter medical school.* I read it with admiration—but it is not the bent of my twig.

65

Sunday afternoon I walk through Westmount to the top of Mount Royal. Lovers, children, puppeteers, gymnasts and assorted exhibitionists. I am driven from my observation post by pangs of hunger. The restaurant is packed, so I grab a bag of french fries and a drink from the hot dog concession. Suddenly a hot dog, all dressed, drops in front of me. Its clumsy owner did not have it properly leashed. Clearing it off the walkway, I throw it into the wastebasket while John Osborne's *Look Back in Anger* falls out of my pocket. *Shall I pretend to be Alison?* asks the woman who dropped her hot dog, picking up my book.

66

The grass is damp; out of her basket comes a blanket. When it is spread out we lie prostrate on it. The material of the blanket is an acute source of frustration. Eventually we are sandwiched under the blanket, shielded from the external world. Suddenly I hear: *Cessez-la, stop that!* I look up to see a mounted policeman.

His horse is doing a restless dance and he rides from couple to couple, sternly uttering his bilingual command.

67

She lives in Hampstead, a student from Sussex who decided to keep house for a Montreal dentist and his family for six months. This is her last week—the family is off for vacation and will return in two days. Then she will travel for a month, mostly in the U.S. We go to the house, which is like a toy castle. There is a small tower at one end, a winding staircase and surprisingly large windows. We attack each other, take off each other's clothes with a desperate sense of urgency. I am being guided to a hitherto unknown destination, along what seems like a long beach of smooth skin, when she disengages and rushes to the bathroom. The door comes half-ajar and I see the lean, beautiful body of a young woman in bloom, small, firm breasts tilting upwards, long legs. And with one leg on the toilet seat she is infusing some white foam into her vagina. I am curious and abashed. Is this a new style of sex from Sussex? Or a recently invented Anglo-Saxon form of sexual perversion? She laughs, seeing me puzzled: *Just some contraceptive stuff,* she says. Soon we both move in an ocean of white foam; a sharp, burning sensation, as if from underground, empties my consciousness of everything except itself.

68

Noises. Startled, I jump out of bed in the middle of the night. The dentist and family return a day early. She hides me in her closet. An hour later, all is quiet. She leads me out of the house. Whispering, we exchange telephone numbers. Next day she calls me. She is packed and on the way to Dorval Airport. I get a cab and pick her up—it is a steady sprinkle, not quite rain. She asks me to go with her; it feels as if she could love me forever.

I can't. At the gate for San Francisco, I leave her. As I walk away I taste the salty tears. Suppressing them, I feel a surge of strange strength, in spite of my immense sadness.

69

Next day I submit my resignation from the job, a month's notice. Then, walking downtown from Verdun, I go and see the Registrar at Sir George. I intend to switch from part-time evening student status to full-time day student. And into the Arts Faculty. I choose a general humanities course and two courses from history and philosophy. The Registrar is not in, but the Assistant Registrar sees me. I am led into an office whose comforts are in stark contrast to the public realms of the institution. He is brusque and has a rather brutal face. He will be with me soon. The shrill tones of what sounds like a marital quarrel filter through the door. Half an hour passes. Feeling faint, I sit in a comfortable leather chair and doze off. The bang of the telephone receiver wakes me and he stands at the door shouting: *Who asked you to sit down?* Calmly, I apologize. In turn, he calms down and apologizes. We conduct the business of transfer. I start my long march through the institutions.

70

A tiny, thin, delicate-looking fellow and I are the best at logic-chopping. Our text is Copi's *Introduction to Logic* and the wealth of exercises provided is overwhelming. We cooperate to get through them and become friends. He is Jean-Paul and his appearance is deceptive—he is tough and disciplined. His room is packed with books. On the wall I read a piece of self-exhortation in huge red letters: "Travaillez, bastard!" I say: *Jean-Paul, when you converse with yourself, must you be so formal? There ought to be at least one person who addresses and treats one in a polite and formal mode,* he answers. I ask him if he can translate what he said into the technical symbolism of formal logic. He does it as well as it can be done. I say: *But Jean-Paul, the "ought" is missing—how are we to construe the "ought"? There is no "ought" in the world,* he claims. *Sometimes it strikes me as if there are too many "oughts" in the world,* I counter. Béla's Ockam's Razor: Oughts should not be multiplied beyond necessity.

71

The special topic in Epistemology is "Our Knowledge of the External World". We are reading A.J. Ayer's book by the same title and John Austin's *Sense and Sensibilia*. The former is tedious, the latter is lively, provocative; its tone is wonderfully set by the ironic literary allusion of its title. Why would you be reading Jane Austen's *Sense and Sensibility* in an epistemology course? After a while, I cease to explain. Austin's lectures are as cheerful as an office boy's whistle; anecdotal, instructive and humourous; full of reminders of our ordinary uses of terms which are misused by philosophers. "Real" is always contrasted with "illusory" in the literature of skepticism. But what about the force of "real" in the remark: That is the real Chinese food? Sam Sigorski sits beside me; he is metaphysically inclined, the self-appointed guru among us. *This is a real pain in the ass. What about that use of "real"?* he whispers. He can recite whole pages from Buber's *I and Thou*. He is wrapped in the halo of mystery and contradiction. Conversations with Sigorski tend to end with Wittgenstein's tautologous dictum: *Whereof one cannot speak, thereof one should be silent.*

72

The "Angel" of epistemology conducts a seminar devoid of discussion. He reads his notes in a distant and cool manner, as if they were someone else's. There is a pause, perhaps to clear the throat. Looking up, he is confronted with a question. Politely hearing it out, he takes his glasses off, cleans his lenses with his tie, then carries on reading his admittedly splendid notes. Could he be taking solipsism too seriously? In any event we meet at cafés for post-seminar discussion, minus Angel. Just next to Sir George, toward Sherbrooke, there is the Tokay Café, and toward St. Catherine there is Carmen. Hungarian is one of the official languages at these cafés; if you place your order in Hungarian, your portions miraculously increase in size, unless you get the rare non-Hungarian waitress. Then you are likely to get the thing you did not order. The topic for our intellectual menu is: How can one know if there are other minds? We shadow-box with the skeptic in us. The strangeness of this venerable problem dawns on me when the waitress interrupts: *Akar még egy kapuccinót?* Without a doubt about her existence, I answer: *Igen,* and then throw myself back into the architecture of our social knowledge and its possibility, without blinking an eye.

73

Tara, dark-eyed to begin with, acquires two gems of green topaz when her interest is aroused. She reads English literature and does the occasional course in philosophy. Her moods are mercurial of late, since she has been abandoned by her boyfriend. *In Praise of Older Women,* says a poster on the wall of the café, an advertisement for Steven Vizinczey's novel. Why older women? Tara is jealous of an abstraction, of a generalization. Jean-Paul: *They are reputed to be more patient, more giving, more possessed of savoir-faire in the ways of love, more understanding of young men. . .* Tara is provoked. Blushing, with her nipples suddenly and conspicuously protruding through her blouse, she rises to the defense of young women everywhere. Jean-Paul chuckles with satisfaction. I am conciliatory: *Well, praising older women does not necessarily imply the denigration of younger women.* She offers me a ride home; the family car is at her disposal. Her parents are vacationing in Florida. We end up in her home; in her room, on her bed, in the nude. I sense that she has a desperate need to prove something—a broad repertoire of techniques, hitherto unknown to me. The delights are bittersweet: I do not seem to be the immediate target of her desire. The room is invaded by others, somehow.

74

Expect the unexpected. Would anyone set anything but an essay question in a philosophy course? In Philosophy, the Last Hundred Years, a course I take, it is a multiple-choice exam. Sample:

The author of the *Tractatus Logico-Philosophicus* and the author of the *Philosophical Investigations*:

a) were identical twins;
b) were brothers;
c) Ludwig Wittgenstein, Jr. and Ludwig Wittgenstein, Sr.;
d) was the dutiful brother who designed his sister's Viennese residence.

The factual nature of the test deflates pretensions but heightens the sense of the absurd.

75

Gloomy, dark and raining. There is a bus strike. Four of us are picked up by a man who insists on surveying our attitudes toward the dismal event: John Kennedy is assassinated. One feels sad, another feels outraged, yet another is in despair. Sigorski feels guilty. The man is perplexed: *How could a person who has not had any involvement with the deed feel guilty?* Sigorski: *Have you heard of the idea of collective guilt? No? Try reading Karl Jaspers's* The Question of German Guilt. *Literature as a weapon*. The man has a German accent. Sigorski is Jewish.

76

Appearance versus reality: by day I am a seemingly indifferent attender of lectures, by evening a café intellectual, by night a very keen student. Hence, a victim of a lack of sleep. Cultivating the appearance of the dilettante yet being a serious student is demanding work. What am I trying to prove? If there is a problem about other minds, surely there is a problem about one's own.

77

Tara takes me to a party. Her boyfriend is there with a woman whose wrinkles are quite beautiful. I have a flash of insight: I am a pawn in a stratagem of sexual revenge. I depart feeling very empty and a bit angry, write a note to Tara, reread Kant's fourth formulation of the Categorical Imperative: "Treat humanity, whether in your own person or in the person of another, never merely as a means but always as an end also. . ." The problem of other minds no longer seems that strange.

78

Mother, Edit and I are reading Canadian history and political structure as a requirement for becoming citizens. The history soon absorbs us, in spite of the frequency of pedestrian and partisan attempts by biased historians to block its fascinating flow. I dream of writing a history of Canada where the phenomena of massacre, courage, conquest and suffering are displayed without the ugly interference and distortions of theory and prejudice; where the dashed hopes and aspirations of the vanquished on the Plains of Abraham are understood rather than dismissed; where the voice of the triumphant victor does not silence the agonized, plaintive voice of the loser. *Öcsi, what naïveté; the voice of history is always the voice of the victor.* Thus, Mother. I see Dr. Budai amidst graves in a cemetery; he is cutting the grass, watering the flowers, caring for the graves. Later, in an impeccable suit, he is guiding visitors through the cemetery.

In front of each grave he stops and pronounces the name and reads the epitaph: *Sullivan, Kennedy, Petöfi, Pearson, Kafka, Hegel, Wittgenstein, Sartre, Camus, Onesi, Wall, Szaba. . . I scream: Who wrote my epitaph?* He chants: *Truth, Beauty and Goodness.* In a monotone, Zen-Buddhist manner. I wake up. It is time for the ceremonies of citizenship.

79

There are about sixty of us in a large hall in a downtown office building. The presiding judge reminds us of the rights and corresponding duties of Canadian citizens. Then, in unison, in different accents, some on the Bible, some on the Koran, we swear allegiance to the Queen. We have a glass of wine at the reception and leave, through Byzantine corridors of the building. I feel relieved and reborn, as if I acquired a very large, valuable possession that I need to maintain and care for. I recall the incongruity of witnessing my own funeral in my dream.

80

Fraser teaches Pragmatism—Pierce, James and Dewey. His shoes are so well polished that I can see my mirror image in them. The lectures have a similar character; the history of philosophy seems to be the chaos of life transfigured into the chaos of diverse intellectual edifices. Some are simple and well lit; others are dark, baroque. Pure reason, by itself, does not redeem anything. I become Spartan, analytical and therapeutic in my approach. How to make an idea clear, how it works in our lives, are questions that loom large in my mind. How can reason allay chaos when it is itself a part of it?

81

Sigorski is asleep. As agreed, I wake him at noon, my shoes soaking with melting snow. No conversation until he has coffee and listens to repeated playings of Gerry and the Pacemakers:

"Don't let the sun catch you crying. . . " We meet Sigorski's girlfriend for lunch. Another girl, with angular features, long brown hair and grey eyes is there: Shauna. She has a striking, aquiline nose and an awkward, somewhat plump body. I have eyes only for her face: I am in love.

82

Equipped with books we baby-sit at Shauna's sister's Westmount house. It is being renovated. She is reading for a psychology examination; I am doing a quick essay for a fellow student on Swift's *A Modest Proposal.* A favour. By midnight we are both rubbing our eyes, exhausted. We fall asleep on the leather couch. Later, stirred by the warmth of her body, I enter her welcoming thighs, open; it is like going home.

83

My favour does not please. The essay I wrote on *A Modest Proposal* receives a B. The fellow student is somewhat enraged. Do I not have a reputation for cleverness? She could have written an essay like this herself! I make an immodest proposal.

84

The screen is covered with the radioactive dust of nuclear fallout. This serves as the bas-relief for the fragility of love and life in *Hiroshima, mon amour.* Shauna and I are frozen in our seats; having expropriated the roles of the lovers, we briefly die with them, resurrected only by the impetus of a pack of pushy fellow students wanting out of the theatre.

85

A faculty member is ill. I am asked to substitute for him. Topic: the Positivist criterion of meaning: "The meaning of a proposition is its method of verification." With a sheath of notes in my hands, I rush to the washroom to urinate. Stage fright. The silence of the classroom is deafening. The chill of death is in the air. I discard my notes and proceed to undress: off with the jacket, loosen the unaccustomed tie. I explore the aims and purposes of the proposed criterion, how it intends to serve as a filter for sense and a discarder of nonsense. And how, in fact, it can be used as a weapon, as a form of violence, as a refusal to understand. There is laughter in the eyes around me. Then I hear: *But what is the meaning of an open fly?* I look down and am confronted with the unzipped fly. Its brute existence destroys the drowsy, weighty seriousness of the lecture. My initial laughter of embarrassment turns into amusement at an incongruous moment. We proceed to have a discussion on the varieties of "meaning".

86

Shauna drags me to a photographer, a surprise photograph for my mother. The photo is enlarged, the blemishes and faults in my face are removed. I am in an academic gown, trying to keep a straight face, for Shauna, behind the photographer's back, lifts her blouse, flaunting her breasts.

87

At the end of term we go for a walk in Notre Dame de Grâce. It is the end of the affair: she wants to marry and she can not marry me. She is Jewish and I am not. Suddenly our world of vast, open space is crowded by ghosts, hovering, singing, chanting incantations and claiming Shauna. Silenced by history, weighed down by tradition, we part.

88

Jean-Paul thinks it best to be a secular saint. Afraid of the rituals and traditions of canonization, I think it best to be a mundane monastic. Further, I don't like the abbreviation SS; MM sounds better. They are the noises children make when munching happily.

89

I apply to Calgary, New Brunswick and McGill to do graduate work in philosophy. My academic record is excellent for the last two years. The professor in charge of admissions for Philosophy graduate students is cold and supercilious. I discern antipathy and dismissiveness in his demeanour. He is as dry as an improperly packaged prune. My hopes to stay in Montréal, close to my family and friends, are dashed. I can not do graduate work without financial assistance.

90

Summer job: at the Sir George Library. It is cramped and chaotic in Circulation. Returned books are to be placed back on the shelves. Dead authors, their voices stifled between the jacket covers, are staring at me in the dimly neon-lit halls, from the shelves. I like to be alone with them, one at a time. Otherwise it is an unseemly chaos.

91

Erika is one of the librarians. By now, her son, cared for during the days by my mother, is grown and ambulatory. He has the most wonderful, large, chestnut-brown eyes. Reciprocity of affection, more like a contagion than a deliberate act, explains why I have the job of "Circulator" from the multitude of applicants. I am befriended by a warm, patient, soothing, articulate female librarian. A New Yorker and a colleague of Erika's. Armed with a long baguette, Mozzarella cheese, Italian salami and a fat bottle of Chianti, we walk up to the mountainside, just a shot away from Sir George. It is sunny, the grass is green and her tenderness is like a sister's. The best thing about public libraries are the librarians!

92

The summer is incredibly hot. I am reading philosophy of history with Dr. Dukelow and six other students. We meet at different restaurants for dinner; the seminar lasts for two to three hours, three times a week. Popper's *The Open Society and Its Enemies* makes a deep impression on me. For some of my heroes, like Plato, appear to be among the enemies. The violence of the other Karl, unfortunately not a member of the Marx Brothers, is more obvious: philosophers have hitherto described the world and the task is to change it. *Je me souviens—la violence.* Yes, change it, but for the better, and this can not be done in terms of rigid schemes and systems, where the voice is privileged, univocal and the source of violence. Perhaps the real revolutionary is he who revolutionizes himself. I incline toward clarification, the dispelling of myth and confusion in the personal life and in the world—my conception is that of a cognitive therapist where the therapist is himself always a therapee, as well.

93

In early June, there is a telephone call from Calgary. A voice says: *Terence Penelhum calling. I am the Head of the Department of Philosophy. I am pleased to be able to offer you a Graduate Fellowship and a Tutorship in Philosophy for the period of twelve months and possibly another year. . . . By the way, how do you pronounce your name? I like to get things right.*

94

Back among the shelves, I suddenly feel the chill of death. I seem to see a volume entitled *Self-Deception* authored by me. "I beseech Thee, unto the bowels of Christ, think it possible you might be mistaken"—this exasperated remark of Oliver Cromwell crosses my mind. Shut up in a room, buried in a book, isolated, away from Mother, Éva, Edit, Gyurka, with thoughts that idle. But they move people; and if they are good, they move them to the good. I think of the wind: it moves the fluffy tops of dandelions. Think of gales and tornadoes: they move houses, tear down trees. . . .

95

*Aleia iacta est.* Jean-Paul and I are at the airport. He is off to Edmonton, I to Calgary. First class, by Air Canada to Winnipeg and then we drive through the prairies. As the plane takes off, desolation overtakes me. I feel Mother's tears, sense a suspicion of betrayal from my sisters. And I am plagued by doubts: can I do any good? Perhaps only if I am not cut off from those I love! As we ascend, the landscape becomes orderly, as if arranged. And then it disappears altogether. I resolve always to stay close enough to see the terrain clearly, never to lose sight of the terrain.